15

MURDER IN IMMUNITY

ANNE CLEELAND

ARTEMIS
PRESS

THE SERIES IN ORDER:

For Daphne Caruana Galizia, who stood up to corruption and paid with her life; and for all others like her.

PROLOGUE

*K*athleen Doyle stared at her companion—a fellow Irishwoman—and made no attempt to hide her immense surprise. *Oh-oh,* she thought, *with a jolt of deep dismay; I wonder what this is all about?* Hesitantly, she replied, "I must say, I'm that gobsmacked."

The two women were standing in the kitchen at Timothy McGonigal's flat, preparing to do the washing-up after their dinner party together. Doyle and her husband had come over, so as to be introduced to McGonigal's latest flame—Georgia Wickham, a lively, clever woman, who was attached to the Irish Embassy, here in London. Shy Tim had been set-up by Father John last Christmas, and this attempt at matchmaking seemed to be working-out well—or, at least it had been working-out well, until the two women had retreated to the privacy of the kitchen, and it suddenly became clear to Doyle that there was a massive storm of trouble brewing.

Seeing her reaction, Doyle's companion leaned against the countertop, and made a wry mouth. "I know it's not necessarily

1

welcome news, and I can hardly blame you. But I wonder if mayhap we could meet-up, soon—just the two of us—and sit down, over a cuppa tea. I'm sure you have some questions."

"Indeed, I do," said Doyle, in all honesty.

"Do you ladies need any help?" interrupted Timothy McGonigal, from the kitchen doorway.

Poor Tim, Doyle thought with a pang, even as she said to him, "Grab an apron, my friend, and roll up your sleeves. You're our only help, because Acton wouldn't have the first idea how to go about it."

"Unfair," Doyle's husband protested, as he joined them in the kitchen. "I'm a fast learner."

"I won't give him anything breakable," the other woman declared, and they all laughed, as people do when they are in the kitchen, and relaxing after an amiable meal.

Tim began to relate an Acton-story from their youth, and Doyle kept her attention firmly fixed on their host, mainly because she could feel her husband's thoughtful gaze, resting upon her. He knows something's upset me, she thought, as she smiled and laughed at Tim's story; I'm an open book, to my better half.

With a casual, unobtrusive movement, Acton moved a bit closer to her side.

CHAPTER 1

*A*cton tucked Doyle's hand into his arm, as they emerged onto the pavement in the posh London neighborhood—quiet, at this time of day, and at this time of year—and began to walk toward where the Range Rover was parked. Progress was necessarily a bit slow, since Doyle was nearing the end of her pregnancy, and it wasn't so very easy to move along, anymore.

In a mild tone, he asked, "Are you going to tell me what she said to you?"

"I am," she replied. "Brace yourself, it's a corker."

"Let's hear it."

Doyle drew in a long breath. "She told me that she's my long-lost aunt. My mother's youngest sister."

At this, he glanced at her, as astonished as he ever allowed himself to be, and she smiled at his reaction. "Told you it was a corker."

"And it isn't true?"

"No, it isn't." Being what the Irish would call "fey," Doyle had an innate ability to read the emotions of the people who were in her presence, and—in particular—she could usually tell when someone was lying. Because she was a detective with Scotland Yard's CID, this talent had come in very useful, in going after the assorted criminals she'd run across. Oftentimes, however, it was a double-edged sword, when it came to friends and acquaintances, and this evening served as a perfect example. They were now sadly aware that Tim McGonigal's new light-o'-love had some sort of scheme, underway— although the particulars of the scheme had yet to be revealed, of course. There were many possibilities, though; Doyle's husband was the wealthy and celebrated Lord Acton, who also happened to be a Chief Inspector with the CID.

Acton lifted his gaze, and took a quick survey of the surrounding area, as they approached their vehicle.

He's wary, she thought; and small blame to him. Into the silence, she offered, "I can't imagine it's about me—it never is —and so I would guess that someone's tryin' to get some sort of leverage over you. She asked if we could get together—just the two of us—and I'd the impression she was hopin' I wouldn't mention it to you, as yet."

"No doubt. She hasn't told McGonigal her tale."

Acton's old friend from university was a genial, kindly man —a respected Harley Street surgeon—but his first loyalty would be to Acton, and he would never have kept this particular secret from him.

They came to the car, and Acton opened her door. "Is there any possibility it is true?"

"No," Doyle said bluntly. "And I was already a bit suspicious, because her accent didn't always stay in place—it

4

was as though she was tryin' to be a bit less posh, than she truly was." With a heartfelt sigh, she added, "Poor Tim."

"Yes."

He came 'round to get into the driver's seat, and was deep in thought, so Doyle respected the process and continued to stay silent, as they drove out into the London night. Acton was an amazing solver-of-crimes, and she could see that he was turning over possibilities in his mind. Unfortunately, someone in his position at the Met would have more than a few enemies —compounded by the undeniable fact that he tended to dabble in questionable activities, himself.

Despite his sterling reputation with the public, Doyle's husband was something of a vigilante, and often arranged matters so that a villain would get his just desserts, outside the safeguards of the justice system. And—to add to her husband's misdeeds—on more than one occasion the renowned Chief Inspector had admired a criminal enterprise so much that he'd taken it over, after throwing the aforesaid criminal in prison— he tended to have a very flexible moral compass, when it came to the fortunes of the House of Acton.

And, because his wedded wife tended to be outraged by such tendencies, he kept his dark doings well-hidden from her —or, at least, he tried to keep them well-hidden. Doyle had an unfair advantage, after all, and so she'd managed to put a stop to more than a few of his questionable impulses. In fact, she was cautiously optimistic that she'd been a good influence on him; Acton had his demons, poor man, and Doyle entertained the shrewd suspicion that those self-same demons were behind his outsized desire to wield control, and take advantage.

But ever since she'd arrived on the scene, and had become his unlikely wife, she'd the sure sense that he was controlling himself a bit better—wasn't taking the terrible chances he used to, when he felt he'd literally nothing to lose. He was never going to abandon his wayward ways—she'd realized, long ago, that he very much enjoyed his masterminding—but at least he was cutting back, and being miles more careful, than he was used. A point to her, all in all, and to his out-sized devotion to her.

Doyle said, "Well, if my Aunty Wickham has been diggin' into my background, you'd best tell me what my records say, before I meet-up with her. I should make sure to get my own story straight."

Doyle had been born to a young, single mother, who'd tangled-up with a nasty character so as to become pregnant with the fair Doyle. Both Doyle's parents were now dead, and Acton had falsified the Dublin records to show that the two had been married, when she was born. Heaven only knew what else he'd falsified; hopefully he hadn't tried to improve her marks at school—the nuns would laugh their heads off.

But he only replied, in no uncertain terms, "You must not meet with her, Kathleen."

Doyle lifted her brows. "D'you think she's dangerous, then?"

He glanced at her. "Do you?"

This, of course, was the more pertinent question, but Doyle slowly shook her head. "I don't have the best record, of knowin' when someone's dangerous, Michael—and I've the bullet wounds, to show for it. But shouldn't we set-up a sting, to find out what's afoot? I could play along—she doesn't know that we've twigged her out, after all."

He was silent, and she could see he was debating whether or not to tell her something. With some exasperation, she advised, "If you know somethin' about what's behind this, Michael, you should tell me."

Slowly, he replied, "I am concerned there may be a connection to the Public Accounts investigation. Ms. Wickham works in the FCDO Building at Whitehall, which is very near the Commission's offices."

A bit taken aback by this implication, Doyle went silent for a moment. They'd recently had a scandal at a local prison, where the prison's administrators had been caught skimming public funds. During that investigation, it had become clear that certain members of the Public Accounts Commission—a Parliamentary agency, which was supposed to act as the watchdog over such things—were instead participating hand-over-fist in the embezzlement scheme.

Because this discovery had broad and troubling ramifications, the Met's investigation into the Public Accounts Commission was ongoing, but had been kept carefully under wraps—although it had necessarily stalled a bit, due to the past month's tragic events. Nevertheless, when the findings were eventually released, there would be a major scandal—along with lengthy prison sentences, for those involved—and so the investigators were treading very carefully.

But—try as she might—Doyle couldn't quite make the leap. "D'you *truly* think there's a connection? Why on earth would the villains send-in a false relative? Seems a very strange thing to do."

But Acton was ever-practical, and only replied, "She does not appear to be irrational, and so we must assume there is a motive, here."

Doyle blew out a breath, and watched as the lamplights passed by, outside her window. "That only makes me want to meet-up with her all the more, Michael. I could do it in a public place—you could hide yourself under the tablecloth, if you're worried."

"Let me think about it," he replied. "I would ask that you make no move, for the time being, and if she attempts to contact you, to let me know immediately."

Reluctantly, she observed, "I suppose we should ask Father John some questions about what she told him, so as to winkle an invitation to Tim's Christmas dinner."

"I would not make mention," he said mildly.

She smiled slightly, in acknowledgement. "Because Father John's a gabbler, born and bred—just like me."

"It is important, for the time being, that she not be made aware that we know she is lying. It would be natural for you to be wary of her claim, in any event, and I think that is the attitude you should take."

Doyle nodded. "All right then—although you'd think that Tim would have twigged her out; he's very protective of you."

"Yes. Which was no doubt why she introduced herself to him through Father John."

"Oh—oh, you're right. Mother a' Mercy, but she's a schemer."

He reached for her hand. "Please don't worry; I will look into it, and—with any luck—discover her motive."

She glanced at him. "Whatever it is, it does seem a bit desperate—seems such a strange tack, to take."

"I would agree."

They lapsed into silence for the remainder of the ride, and Doyle considered this latest development with a great deal of misgiving. It seemed clear that someone was trying to get the upper hand over Acton, which was worrisome in a different way than it should have been, mainly because—in Doyle's experience with such things—any such attempts usually wound up with that person's unplanned trip to the morgue. Her husband wasn't exactly the forgive-and-forget type, and tended to make that sad fact abundantly clear to his enemies. And he'd enemies, of course; he tended to handle high-profile cases with top-shelf criminal types, who would hold a massive grudge—not to mention if word had leaked-out about this Public Accounts investigation, those particular villains would be desperate, indeed, to avoid being exposed, and disgraced.

It just seemed—seemed so *impractical*, that a false aunt would be sent-in to flim-flam the fair Doyle, if that was their plan. But Acton's judgment was sound, and if he thought that was the motivation for this strange turn of events, he wouldn't decide such a thing lightly.

As they rode up the lift from the parking garage to their penthouse flat, she ventured, "I suppose there's no point in askin' you to be careful, Michael, but please keep in mind that if the crooked Commission is behind this, then some powerful people are actin' a bit panicked. You don't want to find out that you're not as bulletproof as you think you are."

She could see that he debated what to say, as they emerged onto the hallway, and began walking toward their door. "I would agree. Which would explain this attempt to find a vulnerability."

The penny dropped, and Doyle could suddenly see his point. Acton might be famous in his own right, but he was also famously devoted to his young Irish wife. He'd been a long-time, reclusive bachelor, and no one was more astonished than Doyle when—out of the blue—her superior officer had proposed marriage, once upon a stake-out. The news media had exploited the Scotland-Yard-romance to the hilt, and the two of them had become the stuff of fairy-tales—the eligible aristocrat, smitten by his Irish Cinderella.

Of course, the fact that Acton was not at all what the public perceived him to be—or that Doyle's fairy-tale marriage was more along the lines of a morality play—was neither here nor there; the pertinent fact remained that Acton was known to dote on his wife, and it seemed entirely plausible that Acton's enemies were trying to create a vulnerability, through his one weakness. Indeed, others had tried such a tactic before, which was why the fair Doyle was always very wary of anyone who suddenly tried to cultivate a friendship with her. It also meant she'd very few trusted friends, but this was not a hardship; she was one who didn't make friends easily, in the first place, and so—in a strange way—she and Acton were perfectly suited.

Her husband put his key card into the slot, but then paused, to lean down and kiss her. "Please don't worry."

"I will worry if I wish," she retorted. "It's my Aunty, after all."

CHAPTER 2

He was behind it, of course. It seemed that he was tired of the stand-off, and had decided to escalate. His goal, however, was unclear.

Reynolds, their butler, greeted them at the door, and then took their coats, as Doyle asked, "How was Edward?" Edward was their young son, and the butler had been tasked with watching him tonight, since Callie, their nanny, was out on loan.

"Master Edward was his usual irrepressible self, madam," Reynolds replied smoothly.

"Sorry," said Doyle. "Did you have to lock yourself in the lift?"

"Certainly not, madam; I hit upon a plan to go on a treasure hunt, to find raisins."

Doyle smiled. "Good thinkin'. How many times did you have to read *The Gingerbread Man*?" As was often the case with children his age, Edward was obsessed with a book—one that featured the nursery rhyme about the elusive gingerbread man.

"Only twice, madam."

"Well, I would love to hide the wretched book, save that I fear the melt-down that would follow. You've earned your day off tomorrow, Reynolds; thank you."

"It was my pleasure, madam; might I prepare a nightcap, sir?"

"No, thank you, Reynolds; but I would ask that you visit my office, before you retire."

Oh-oh, thought Doyle. That doesn't sound good; my husband wants to speak to Reynolds, without the wife of his bosom, listening in.

Acton offered an arm to assist her down the stairway to the lower floor, and as she navigated the steps, she asked in a low tone, "What's to do?"

He explained, "We were scheduled to have the new nanny from the agency come for a try-out, tomorrow, but I will ask Reynolds if he will cancel her, and instead work an extra day."

She glanced up at him. "That's a bit ominous, Michael."

"Only a precaution," he assured her, and it was the truth. "Reynolds vetted her, and I did a background check. There was nothing alarming, but—in light of this evening's developments —I would like to err on the side of caution, and push-off anyone new, for a few days."

Doyle offered, "I can always stay home with the boyo, Michael; I'm only goin' in as an assist, anyways." Due to her impending maternity leave, Doyle was no longer formally assigned to any cases, but was instead assisting other officers, on an as-needed basis.

But his response surprised her. "No; I think it is important that you report as scheduled, and follow your usual routine. Ms. Wickham must not be made aware that you are skeptical of her claim."

Nodding, she agreed, "Aye then. I was plannin' to go by, and have a visit with Mary on my way in to headquarters tomorrow—is that all right, still?"

"By all means."

Mary, their usual nanny, was currently taking her own maternity leave, and—in an ironic twist—Callie, the young woman who was supposed to be helping Doyle in the meantime, had been loaned out to new-mother Mary, who was needing all the help her friends could muster.

He added, "I believe Lizzie Williams will be at Mary's also, tomorrow morning."

"Good," Doyle replied. "Lizzie's just what Mary needs, to help her with the wee lass—someone who's capable, and no-nonsense."

Lizzie was a forensics tech at the Met, and another—like Callie, the young nanny—who'd been hired due to their long-time connection to the House of Acton—both having formerly worked at Trestles, Acton's hereditary estate.

It was all a bit strange, and hard to fathom for Doyle, who couldn't understand why anyone would hold a loyalty to any particular bloodline—especially a loyalty that seemed to trump all other considerations. But the allegiance was undeniable, and Doyle had seen it in action, on more than one occasion. Of course, that loyalty also meant that Acton could trust his retainers to serve his interests, and his alone—which came in very handy, being as many of his interests couldn't withstand the light of day.

They came into their bedroom, and as Acton turned on the

light, Doyle gratefully sank onto the bed, kicking the shoes off her swollen feet. Acton stood for a moment, gazing out the windows at the park lights, far below. "How does Mary's baby?"

"Hannah, she is." Doyle paused, for a poignant moment. "Sweet Hannah." With an effort, she shook off her sadness, and teased, "Gear up, my friend; I'm goin' to want a girl, sooner or later." This, because their second child was slated to be a boy.

He turned to her, responding to her teasing with his own smile. "I shall do my best."

"You always do." This, said with a great deal of meaning.

He leaned down to kiss her temple. "Hold that thought; I must go speak with Reynolds."

"And you're dyin' to do some research about my false Aunty—there's no need to pretend otherwise, husband. I'll not see you 'till the wee hours, and it's a shame I haven't a boyfriend, that I could ring-up at times like this."

"I don't know as you're in any shape to entertain a boyfriend," he pointed out reasonably.

"Don't make it a challenge, else I'll phone the night-shift Desk Sergeant, here and now."

He tilted his head in apology. "It is important that I discover who she is, and who she associates with."

"A'course—I'm only teasin', Michael; just remember to get some rest." She paused, thoughtfully. "She might be from Midlands, somewhere, if I were guessin'."

He raised his brows. "Anything else?"

"Not religious-minded—although I suppose that goes without sayin', if she's tryin' to pull one over. I made a reference to Candlemas Day, and she hadn't the first idea what I was talkin' about." She paused, suddenly struck. "D'you think our Ms. Wickham is connected to Charbonneau? Charbonneau might be someone who's lookin' for leverage over you."

The point-man—or point-woman, more correctly—in the prison embezzlement scheme was a woman named Charbonneau, who'd played least-in-sight, ever since the CID had rolled-up that rig. And, now that the wrongdoing had been traced to the Public Accounts Commission, Doyle knew that the investigators were very interested in taking a hard look at Charbonneau's dealings, being as it appeared that she'd acted as the main liaison between the villains on the Commission, and the various public entities that were being embezzled.

So far, however, they were having trouble building a case against the elusive woman—which was something of a surprise to Doyle, since when she'd met Charbonneau at the prison, she didn't get the impression that the woman was clever enough to outsmart the police. And—to make it doubly-embarrassing—Charbonneau was a "CI"—a Confidential Informant, used by the Met to gather information from other criminals, so as to quietly pass it on to law enforcement. The fact that the Met was having trouble locating her did not speak very well, for the CI Unit.

"It is entirely possible that Ms. Wickham is connected, in some way, to Charbonneau," Acton agreed, and Doyle had the immediate impression he'd already entertained this suspicion.

This was a troubling development, because if Charbonneau was indeed the one behind Doyle's false aunt, it would indicate that word was leaking out about the Public Accounts investigation, even though the investigators were trying to keep it carefully under wraps. Aunty Wickham may have been sent-in to find out how much was known.

Reaching for his hand, she kissed its back. "Wake me, if you decide we've got to strap-on some Kevlar."

"I'm not sure your vest would fit," he pointed out. "I would have to give you mine."

"Always the gentleman," she declared with great fondness, as he closed the door behind him.

CHAPTER 3

*T*he following morning saw Doyle at Mary-the-nanny's flat, which was located in a posh building, a few blocks away from where Doyle lived. Of course, how much longer Mary would be able to remain in this posh building was a good question—but one hurdle at a time, as Doyle's mother always used to say.

Reynolds had packed-up breakfast pastries for her visit, and as Lizzie Williams made tea in the kitchen, Doyle sat down next to Mary on the sofa, watching as she breast-fed her new daughter. The curtains were opened, this time, and Doyle—always sensitive to atmosphere—decided that everything felt a bit lighter, this visit. She was a true believer, was Mary, and she'd already shown herself to be resilient against life's heavy blows—although it did seem that she'd weathered more than her fair share.

I don't know how I would hold up, if I were in her

situation, Doyle thought, and then immediately decided not to think about it.

Instead, she leaned in to run a gentle hand over the fine, blonde fuzz on the back of the baby's head. "How are you, today, Mary? Although you're probably pig-sick of people askin'."

Lizzie came over to serve the pastry tray, and Doyle smiled her thanks, as Mary replied, "Not at all, Lady Acton—I appreciate your asking. I am getting better, every day. It's the adjusting, that's hard, but I've only to find my feet, again."

Doyle nodded. "Aye, it's what Sister Luke used to call 'the precious ordinary'; the blessin' of borin', routine days—that we don't appreciate at all—until they're suddenly taken away, and then we'd do anythin', just to have them back again."

"Exactly," Mary agreed, with a faint smile. But we have to trust in God—know that the Redeemer lives."

Doyle quirked her mouth. "Easier said than done, sometimes."

They sat together in silence for a few moments, and then chuckled when the baby made a smacking sound.

"She's thrivin'," Doyle offered.

"She's a miracle," said Mary, her voice breaking a bit.

The tears came, and Doyle moved to awkwardly embrace the other woman—not easy, with her pregnant tummy in the way, and the baby annoyed that she was being squashed.

"Sorry," said Mary after a few moments, as she took a deep breath, and straightened up.

"Whist, Mary; you're entitled. How go the sessions with Father John?"

"He's so comforting—so steady," the other said, wiping her

eyes with a napkin. "I go counsel with him, every morning, after Mass. Philippe takes me."

Doyle blinked. "Philippe Savoie?"

Smiling at Doyle's reaction, Mary nodded. "Yes—Mr. Savoie. First, we drop off Emile and Gemma at school, and then he drives me over to St. Michael's. He's been very good, and he insists that I call him 'Philippe,' because he says we're friends." She paused to confess, "It does feel a bit strange."

"It's not an easy name," Doyle observed. "Doesn't roll off the tongue, for us English-speakin' types."

"No—and he calls Hannah '*chou-chou*', which is apparently something they call babies in France. He holds her in the pew, when I go in to counsel with Father John."

A bit guiltily, Doyle offered, "Well, if you need someone else to take you over, I'll be happy to, Mary. I didn't realize you were goin' to daily Mass, and shame on me, for not offerin' sooner."

But Mary only disclaimed, "No—it works out well, since the children have to be driven to school, anyway, with the weather still so cold."

A bit bemused, Doyle considered the extraordinary fact that someone like Philippe Savoie was willing to step up, in this time of crisis. Savoie—to put it plainly—was something of an criminal kingpin; a French kingpin, who'd nonetheless managed to save the fair Doyle's life, once upon a disaster—twice, actually, if you toted them up—and so, Acton tolerated the man's presence in their lives, despite the fact that a Chief Inspector probably shouldn't be consorting with notorious French criminals.

From what Doyle had gleaned, Savoie had been running several lucrative smuggling rigs on the Continent, until he'd come to England, on the suspicion that he was being double-crossed by his Russian partner-in-crime. Then—after the Russian kingpin's untimely death—Savoie had adopted the dead man's small son, and had named him Emile, after Savoie's own dead brother.

It was an extraordinary turn of events, but even more extraordinary was the fact that Doyle suspected Acton had enlisted Savoie in some of his own questionable activities—although the two men were careful not to be seen together, and Acton scrupulously hid any hints of such an alliance from the fair Doyle.

Doyle wasn't fooled, but there wasn't much she could do about it; she owed Savoie her life, twice over—and besides, she and Savoie were friends, in a strange way.

And now, Savoie's son Emile was fast-friends with Mary's little girl, Gemma, who went to the same school as the boy. It was all very symmetrical—the way their lives had become intertwined—and Doyle decided that she shouldn't be surprised that Savoie had, yet again, shown that he had hidden depths, and wasn't half so ruthless as he appeared.

Mary smiled at Doyle. "Nonsense; you've already done plenty, Lady Acton. I so appreciate Callie, and Lizzie."

Reminded, Doyle glanced over toward the nursery, where Lizzie was moving about the room, straightening-up. "Where's our Callie—is she out runnin' errands?"

"No—Callie couldn't come in, today."

This was rather a surprise, since the House of Acton was paying the young nanny to help the widow out, in this time of need. Doyle ventured, "She's not sick, or anythin'?"

"No, she called this morning to ask if it would be all right."

Mary made a sound of sympathy. "She's a young girl, after all, and I think it's all a bit upsetting, for her."

"Aye, that," Doyle agreed. "She's been so steady, though; I'm surprised she took Dutch-leave without sayin' somethin' to me, first—she knows you're not one to raise an objection."

Mary raised her brows in alarm. "Oh—please don't let me get her into trouble, Lady Acton. I'm doing much better—I really don't even need Lizzie, anymore."

Glancing again toward the nursery, Doyle lowered her voice in amusement. "Lizzie must be wonderin' what hit her, what with two wee babies to manage, all in the course of a few months."

Lizzie had married Thomas Williams, one of Doyle's fellow detectives at Scotland Yard, only to discover that her new husband had fathered a child, unbeknownst to him. Since the mother was now dead, the couple had adopted the unexpected baby, and were coping with their instant-family as best they could.

Mary chuckled. "It goes to show that you never know, do you?"

Doyle smiled in response. "No—you definitely don't, and I'm the poster-child for such things. Let's keep Lizzie comin' in the mornin's, for the time bein'. She's not one to be underfoot."

"Not at all," Mary agreed. "Which is a blessing, really. I don't always feel like talking to someone, and she's not a talker."

"Oh-oh," said Doyle, with an exaggerated show of guilt. "I should take my leave, then."

"You know I didn't mean you," Mary protested, with a smile. She then lowered her voice, still further. "Lizzie did ask about

Nigel, though—about his medication. I think she's worried I didn't give it all to the police." She paused, and then added fairly, "I've been a bit scatterbrained, but not *that* scatterbrained."

Suddenly all attention, Doyle asked in a casual tone, "Oh? What did she ask?"

Mary shifted the baby to her shoulder, and began to pat her back. "How long he'd been taking it—quite some time, of course, since he'd hurt his back in the army." At this, she paused, blinking back tears for a moment, and then added, "I should go through his things, but I can't quite bring myself to do it, yet."

Doyle covered the other woman's hand with her own, and said firmly, "You will do nothin' you don't wish to, Mary— d'you hear me? You've plenty of time, and no reason to rush. And I'll be happy to help you, when the time comes." Reminded, she added, "And let me know, if you need Acton to speak to the building's management about stayin' on; no need to uproot poor Gemma, after all—she's lived through enough changes, already."

"Thank you, Lady Acton, but you needn't worry—I telephoned them to ask, but they told me that Nigel had paid the rental, all the way through to the end of the year."

"Oh—well, that's a relief," said Doyle, and kept her conclusions to herself. Bless that husband of mine, she thought, and not for the first time; he's always one step ahead of me.

CHAPTER 4

*O*nce her visit was over, Doyle texted the driving-service, which was provided by their fancy residential building. She wasn't the best driver, and Acton had expressed his preference, early-on, that she use the driving service, whenever she needed to navigate the London streets.

She'd been reluctant, at first, to be ferried about in a limousine—as though she were putting on airs—but she'd long been reconciled, since it gave her a few minutes to relax in quiet, and to think over whatever she needed to do next—she was never very organized, which was a decided drawback, with this sort of work.

As soon as she was settled into the back seat—no easy task, to buckle a seatbelt, nowadays—Doyle rang up her husband on their private line.

He answered immediately, as he always did. "Kathleen."

"Don't die," she instructed.

"Right, then; I won't. How did she seem?"

Doyle sighed. "Better. I got her to chuckle, a few times."

"None more able."

She smiled, aware that he was trying to cheer her up. "Well, I can make the devil laugh at a christenin'; it's one of my few talents."

"There are some other talents I might name."

"Not that you were at all interested, last night. I'm the size of a walrus, and I've lost all my allure."

"Not at all; it took a great deal of resistance, I assure you."

She smiled into the phone. "You do turn a girl up sweet, Michael. What do we know about my Aunty?"

"Not much. Her records appear to have been scrubbed."

Doyle paused, thinking this over. "Well, that's not good—you were right; she must be connected to the Public Accounts case." This, because if Wickham was able to hide her records from Acton—who was a wizard, at digging things up—it meant that she was either very tech-savvy—which seemed unlikely—or she'd some very powerful people, backing her attempt to breach fortress-Acton.

"I would imagine that is the case, yes."

"I'm still a bit murky on all this," Doyle admitted. "What would be the point, of my Aunty's wormin' her way into my good graces? Information? I'm not assigned to the Public Accounts case, and it's not like you're goin' to unbutton, to the likes of her."

"Very true. Her motives are as yet unclear, and for that reason you must be careful; she may try to approach you in a public place, so as to compel you to be polite, and sit down with her."

Doyle offered doubtfully, "I don't know as anyone can compel me to be polite, Michael."

She could sense his smile. "Very true. She wouldn't know this, though."

"If it does happen, what should I say to her? Or should I just take her down in a chokehold, and have done?"

"Agree to meet, but push her off for a few days, until I can discover more. You would be naturally wary, and you should convey that attitude."

"Right; no love lost, between me and my mum's family, after all—they ditched her without a backward glance. Have you asked Tim about her?"

"Not as yet."

She grimaced into the phone. "Aye; that's a bit tricky, isn't it? The moment you start askin' questions about her, Tim's goin' to know that somethin's up—he's no fool."

"Yes."

"He'll drop her like a shot—he's very protective of you."

"And I should be protective of him, in turn."

"Good point, of course—we can't leave him in the dark. Poor man; he has the worst luck."

"I must go, I'm afraid."

"All right; let me know the minute you find out anythin' of interest—I'm all on end."

"I will. I am scheduled for a task-force meeting this morning, but I should have more to report when we visit Dr. Easton."

"Oh—that's right; my wretched doctor's appointment."

Because she was now in the final stages, Doyle had to go see her stupid obstetrician every week, which only added insult to the beached-walrus injury. "See you then." She teetered on the edge of mentioning her appreciation, that he'd thought to pay for Mary's rental, but then decided to refrain;

he hadn't mentioned it, himself, and such a good deed could keep.

She rang off, and gazed out the window at the passing scenery for a moment, thinking about this rather ominous development—that the wretched Ms. Wickham was someone who knew how to hide her background from an expert. The woman seemed harmless enough, but—obviously—she'd some fell purpose, in mind; if the blacklegs had got wind that the great Chief Inspector Acton was scrutinizing them, they'd be very nervous bureaucrats, and rightly so. Still, it seemed a strange and convoluted tack to take, if their object was to extract information from the fair Doyle, about the status of her husband's investigation.

And—speaking of such—she'd forgot to ask him what Lizzie's purpose was, in asking Mary about her deceased husband's medications. Presumably, Acton was the one who was truly asking the questions, not Lizzie, which must mean that he'd some unresolved concerns about the tainted-medication case.

Which seemed a bit odd, since the tainted-medication case was now closed, and it hadn't even been Acton's case, to being with. A batch of common medication that was used for chronic pain had been tainted with fentanyl, and within a day, ten people living in London had died from an overdose—Nigel Howard, Mary's husband, being the most prominent of the victims. Howard was an MP, and had tragically collapsed, even as he was enacting business at the Parliament building.

The appropriate regulatory agency had immediately traced the tainted medication to a certain batch, and there was now a massive regulatory investigation, going forward, over standards and processing practices—with the public outraged, as of course they should be. Nobody liked to think that an innocuous dose of medicine could be fatal, due to the processor's negligence.

So; that seemed a bit odd—that Lizzie was seeking-out information about Nigel Howard's use of the drug, and that she was presumably doing it at Acton's request. Although it could be that Doyle was jumping to the wrong conclusion; mayhap it was only exactly what it seemed, and Lizzie was truly worried that Mary hadn't given the police all of Howard's medication—Mary wasn't in any shape to be thinking clearly, poor thing.

As Doyle stared out the car window, her scalp started prickling, which is what it did when her intuition was demanding that she pay attention—although it wasn't always easy to pay attention, when one was suffering from the latter stages of pregnant-brain.

Thus prompted, she remembered that Mary had made another comment, that had caused the fair Doyle's antenna to quiver, which meant she should probably follow-up on that one, too.

Shifting her girth, she leaned forward to open the privacy panel, and speak to Adrian, the driver. "How are you, Adrian?"

Adrian was another loyal foot-soldier who'd originated from the town near Acton's estate—along with Lizzie and Callie. It was a tight-knit group, and they all knew each other from their childhoods. In fact, Doyle had gained the impression that Adrian was rather sweet on Callie, which was one of the reasons she wished to speak with him.

The driver flashed his white smile into the rear-view mirror. "I am fine, Lady Acton."

"Well, I imagine you've your finger on the pulse of all

things Callie, and so unsnabble, and tell me why she didn't show up at Mary's, this mornin'."

His expression immediately fell a bit, and he offered, "I don't know, ma'am. She didn't tell me anything."

Doyle ventured, "She seems a bit down-pin, lately."

He tilted his head in commiseration. "She's shaken-up, finding out about her birth-mother. She's trying to sort it all out."

"Aye—there's nothin' like a long-lost relative, to shake you up," Doyle agreed thoughtfully. Callie was adopted, and had recently discovered that her birth mother was Melinda Clarence, an aristocratic woman from an estate that neighbored Acton's. In a strange twist of fate, it turned out that Acton's father had also been her father, so that Acton and Callie were half-siblings.

With a casual air, Doyle suggested, "Mayhap you should track her down, and take her out for an ice cream, or somethin', after work—there's that little shop near Mary's, remember? She may have need of a listenin' ear."

Adrian—who was too polite to show that he was wise to Doyle's clumsy attempts at matchmaking, replied, "That's a good idea, ma'am—although I think she's trying to get over a breakup, too."

Amazed, Doyle stared at the back of his head. "Callie had a *boyfriend*? Faith, I never heard a whisper about it."

"She kept it very quiet, ma'am. I think she really liked him."

Oh-oh, thought Doyle; he's worried, is our Adrian, and I should probably shake my stumps, and find out why.

But before she could delve any further, they'd pulled up to the pavement in front of headquarters, and Doyle decided that it would have to wait.

CHAPTER 5

he Colonel's killing had been a concern.

There would have to have been good reason not to defer to him, and tell him ahead of time what had been planned, and that reason seemed clear; Savoie wanted leverage.

But why? They had encountered no problems, in their dealings, and the Frenchman knew better than to try to cheat him.

And so, wary, he'd watched, and listened, and tried to discern the man's motivation, in seeking-out such leverage.

And then—with some wonder—he'd finally realized what that motivation was. In his own defense, it was not something anyone would have guessed.

He realized that there had already been one attempt to eliminate the husband, and so—to ward-off any further such attempts—he'd encouraged an alliance with his half-sister, who was willing, because she already admired the man.

This had a two-fold purpose; to send a warning that he knew what was intended, and, at the same time, to offer an acceptable compromise.

If Savoie had been a fellow peer, he'd have been flattered by the proposal, even if he'd turned it down. But instead—apparently—the offer had enraged him. And he was a dangerous man, when enraged.

CHAPTER 6

*D*oyle knocked on the door jamb of Detective Inspector Thomas Williams' office, and then leaned-in to announce, "Acton's pushin' my pregnant self off on you, because poor Munoz is sick to the back teeth of me, and now it's your turn."

Williams glanced up from where he was seated at his desk. "Always a pleasure, Kath. We'll be seeing Munoz this morning, anyway, since she's on-site at the new case, and I'm the SIO." He closed his desk laptop, and then rose to get his suit jacket from the hanger on the back of the door.

"Remind me what this one's about." Doyle hadn't read-up on this morning's new homicide case, mainly because she wasn't good at paying attention to multiple things—even when she wasn't pregnant—and between Mary's tragedy and the false-Aunty situation, her poor brain was overburdened.

"It seems to be fairly straightforward case of graveyard-love. We got a tip about a domestic situation from a neighbor, but before Dispatch could send a field unit out for a welfare-check, the man killed the woman, and then himself."

"Ach," Doyle said. "Such a shame." Graveyard-love was the term the police used for someone who'd rather murder the object of his or her affections than see them walk out the door.

Williams nodded, as they walked together down the hallway. "We'll see what the story is, but it's probably the usual."

"The usual" was some poor woman being subjected to escalating abuse by her partner or husband, and then finally deciding that she'd had enough and was leaving—to the deadly fury of the aforesaid partner.

"I hope there aren't any children involved," Doyle remarked, as they paused before the lift.

"If there are, they're probably better off out of that situation, Kath."

But she blew out a breath. "Whist, Williams; the last needful thing is to grow up with the knowledge that your da killed your mum."

He shrugged a shoulder. "But imagine the misery they saw, in their day-to-day lives. That's not healthy, either."

"I'll concede you have a point, my friend, and speakin' of such, how's the boyo?" Williams and his wife, Lizzie, had recently adopted the baby boy who was the result of his one-night stand, before they were married.

Williams smiled his rare, genuine smile, as he pulled up a snap of the baby to show her. "He's doing great, although I don't think I'm ever going to get a good night's sleep again."

Doyle winced. "Don't remind me; it's brutal, and I'm about to gird-up my loins and charge back in, myself."

He cocked a skeptical brow, as he sheathed his phone. "You have nannies, though."

"Not at night, my friend. I'm on the clock at night, with only the occasional assist from Acton."

Surprised, he said, "Really? You'd think that's when you'd need a nanny the most."

But she replied thoughtfully, "I don't know; I like to sit there, in the dark, quiet, house—just the two of us. It's as though you're alone in the universe, together. It's worth the sacrifice of sleep."

He smiled, as they stepped into the lift. "I know—I like that feeling, too. And I have to help out—poor Lizzie is so tired. She's helping Mary, and trying to get some work done, too. Acton has her working on multiple cases, in the lab. He's sorry for it, but he doesn't trust anyone else."

Doyle nodded, well-aware of how Acton had Lizzie working on his own, off-the-books pursuits, on top of her normal caseload at the CID. "And it doesn't help matters, that Callie was playin' least-in-sight, this mornin'." Glancing at him sidelong, she ventured, "Has Lizzie said anythin' about Callie's big news?"

"Yes. I didn't have the impression that it was much of a secret."

"No, and it shouldn't be—there's no shame to fall on her, after all. And since everyone now knows that she'd related to Acton, she'll definitely have more options, despite her bein' a by-blow."

He laughed aloud. "Now, there's an old-fashioned word."

She smiled. "In Ireland, we'd say that you're a gooseberry-baby."

"Well, then Connor's a gooseberry-baby, too. We're already

stressing about how much to tell him, when the time comes—it's not as though his real mother wasn't completely mad."

Doyle made a sound of commiseration, because Callie's true father—Acton's father—had also been completely mad. "I'll grant you that it's a minefield, and I can see your point—even though I'm not one for secrets; secret-keepin' always seems to lead to trouble."

He smiled. "That's because no one can have a secret, around you."

Williams was the only other person—save Acton—whom she'd told about her perceptive abilities, even though Acton felt very strongly that she shouldn't ever tell anyone. She trusted Williams, though, and at the time, it was important to let him know that a young woman was leading him astray.

Absently, she replied, "That's not always true, my friend; Acton has a bushelful of secrets, that he keeps from me." Oh, she thought in some surprise; now, where did that thought come from?

But her companion only said, "Don't put me in a divided-loyalties situation, Kath."

"Oh—oh, right; sorry."

The lift doors slid open, and they began to walk through the parking garage. Williams was yet another one who assisted Acton in his questionable pursuits, and—since he and Doyle were good friends—they'd decided long ago that they'd best avoid trying to ferret-out what the other knew about Acton's doings, since neither of them wanted to be placed in a divided-loyalties situation.

Willing to change the subject, she offered, "Well, wait 'till you hear this; it turns out Tim McGonigal's sweetheart is tryin' to convince me that she's my long-lost aunt."

Her companion turned to stare at her in abject surprise. "*Is* she?"

"Oh, yes, my friend; we'd a dinner party at his flat last night, and she sidled up to drop the news."

He chuckled, as he opened the car door for her. "It's funny, really, that she'd try to pull the wool over on you, without realizing you'd see right through her."

She made a face. "Not so funny, in truth; it all seems a bit ominous, and Acton thinks she may be connected to the Public Accounts case."

He gave a low whistle. "Really? What's the gambit? She's hoping to obtain information?"

Doyle raised her palms, as he started the car. "I don't know, but it seems unlikely that she truly thinks she'd get anything useful, from me—I'm not handlin' the case, and I'm about to go on maternity leave, at any minute. I can't imagine that she thinks she can try to wheedle Acton—he's wheedle-proof."

"Leverage?" he mused. "She's been sent-in to try to find something to hold over your heads?"

She shot him a look. "Good luck to her."

He smiled in appreciation. "Obviously, she doesn't know who she's dealing with."

"Aye; she'll only reap the whirlwind. I almost feel sorry for her, to be so cow-handed, and naïve."

As he drove out of the structure, he suggested, "Let's try a different working-theory; could she be just an ordinary grifter, hoping for a payout?"

But Doyle shook her head. "That's not a very good theory, either—what did she think—that Acton was goin' to throw open the vault? Again, it seems so naïve—even as you have to admire someone who has the brass neck to even try it."

"Well, she obviously doesn't know you as well as she pretends; aside from your—your talent, you're very protective of Acton."

"That's true." Teasing, she glanced over at him. "And of you, too."

He ducked his chin in acknowledgment. "Don't think I'm not grateful."

"Well, I never had a brother, but you're how a brother would be, I think."

"Great," he said, with heavy irony. "If you'd only mentioned that at the first, it would have saved me a lot of trouble and heartache."

He could joke about it, now, but when they'd first met, poor Williams had carried quite the torch for the fair Doyle, and her unexpected marriage to the Chief Inspector had thrown him into a tailspin. And then, there'd been an occasion or two when Williams had made some bad decisions, but he'd been saved from Acton's wrath, mainly because he was one of Doyle's few friends. In a strange way, Williams had immunity, due to his friendship with Doyle.

Suddenly, she stilled. Oh, she realized; oh—I think that's it. My false aunt must be an attempt by the blacklegs to gain immunity—immunity from the hellfire that's about to rain down upon their heads. They must be aware that Acton's quietly on the case, and so they're spooked to pieces. And if they can convince me that my only known relative is involved in the mess, that might prevent the hammer of justice from banging down—or at least, it would soften the blow. There's the motive, clear as day, and I imagine Acton has already come to this conclusion, since he's always ten steps ahead of me.

"What's Acton going to do about her? Get a restraining

order?"

Recalled to the conversation, she warned, "I'm not sure—I think he's not sure, either. Don't say anythin'."

"I won't." Williams added, "He's not going to be kind."

"No, he's not; which—again—just shows you that she hasn't done her homework. It's not as though he was goin' to fall on her neck, and weep; he doesn't much like the relatives he already has."

"Relatives can cut both ways," Williams agreed. "I had a nasty uncle, remember."

"So you did; I'd forgot."

Williams had discovered that his uncle had molested and then killed his cousin, and so he and Acton had served-out a bit of justice, with no one the wiser.

Her companion pronounced grimly, "If anyone tried anything like that with Connor, he'd be equally dead."

Annoyed, she scolded, "Murder's never the answer, Thomas; I've told you a *million* times."

"Sometimes, it is."

To change the subject—this was old ground, and they weren't going to agree, after all—she remarked, "Well, just wait until Connor is obsessed with a book, and won't let you read anythin' else. Murder does come to mind—faith, but I'm pig-sick, of the stupid gingerbread man."

He laughed. *"Run, run, fast as you can—you can't catch me, I'm the gingerbread man."*

"If I never hear it again, it will be too soon."

"I used to love *Peter Rabbit*. I can't wait till Connor's old enough."

"It will be a mixed blessin', believe me."

They drove for a few moments in companionable silence,

until he glanced her way. "Didn't you have a walk-in, this morning? What did she want?"

Doyle grimaced. "I'm meetin' with her later today, actually —I can't put her off, anymore. The Desk-Sergeant said he tried to refer her to the tip-line, but she insisted on speakin' with me in person."

Williams gave her a sympathetic look, because this did not bode well; if a volunteer witness showed up out of the blue, oftentimes it was someone who was looking for attention —"kook detail," they called it—although not everyone was a kook, of course. But usually, if a tipster had a tip, they would just phone the tip-line, so as to remain anonymous, and shield themselves from any further involvement. Those who insisted on coming in to headquarters were usually the attention-seekers—not to mention that this one had asked for Officer Doyle, in particular. Doyle was something of a folk-hero to the public, in that she'd once jumped into the river Thames to save a colleague, even though she couldn't swim. And so—for many people—hers was the only name at the Met that they knew.

He offered, "It might be something worthwhile—you never know."

"Aye—I should have a better attitude. My hat's off to the tip-line people, for having to deal with it on a regular basis."

"It's a mutual-admiration thing, then; Mallory from the tip-line is one of your biggest fans. She was asking me about you, the other day."

Doyle teased, "Be careful, or Lizzie will take an edged-weapon to the fair Mallory."

He chuckled. "I don't think Lizzie's the jealous type, Kath."

Doyle held her tongue, and looked out the window as she yet again contemplated the general cluelessness of men.

CHAPTER 7

$\mathcal{D}$oyle followed Williams into the crime scene, ducking under the tape, and greeting the field officer who'd been posted on the perimeter. The place was a walk-up in a modest building in Camden, and Detective Sergeant Isabel Munoz stood at the doorway awaiting them, alongside Detective Constable Jerry Shandera.

"What's the report, Sergeant?" asked Williams, as both he and Doyle peered beyond them, into the small utility flat.

Munoz replied, "Two DBs, sir; male and female, with fatal gunshot wounds. The Coroner thinks time-of-death for both is around nineteen-hundred."

Williams nodded. "Do we have IDs?"

"Yes; Rosanna Diaz and Enrique Valdez. She's listed at this address, but he's not; neither are married. Had a tip-line report from yesterday that they were loudly quarreling. Her suitcase is laid out on the bed."

"Thank you; let's have a look."

Williams walked into the flat with Munoz, over to where the SOCO photographer was taking some last, follow-up snaps. Doyle hung back in the doorway, because the fewer the people on-site, the better for evidence recovery, and besides, it seemed fairly obvious what had happened. The female victim had a gunshot wound to the upper chest, and had bled out, clutching the kitchen counter for a time before she collapsed to the floor, as was evidenced by the bloody handprints along the cabinets.

The male victim had retreated toward the window, and was lying face-up, with an entry-wound on his right temple. He'd crumpled to the floor, his head at that awkward angle that resulted when someone had lost all muscle function, all at once. His gun had dropped to the floor, near to his right hand. Graveyard-love; a murder-suicide, because one party couldn't bear the thought of being left by the other.

"Illegal weapon?" Williams asked Munoz, as a matter of form. It was rare for anyone to legally own a gun, in Britain.

"No, sir; he's licensed, because he's a transport guard."

Williams raised his brows, considering this. "Is there a mobile? Have we had a look at his texts?"

Officer Shandera replied, "Not as yet, sir. There was a mobile on the counter, but it was locked."

"How about her?"

"No mobile on site," Shandera said.

That's odd, thought Doyle. If she lived here, you'd think her mobile would be here.

Shandera offered, "Shall I put-in a request to the phone company for her records, sir?"

Williams glanced up at him, from where he crouched. "Let's hold off; it may not be necessary."

"Yes, sir."

Williams then stood, and began conferring with the SOCOs, whilst Munoz retreated back to stand near Doyle. Doyle took the opportunity to say to the other detective in an undertone, "I don't know as I like this, Munoz."

Munoz nodded. "No, me neither. It looks as though she was making a *tombet.*"

"Oh?" Doyle regarded the various vegetables, arrayed along the countertop.

Munoz indicated with a nod. "See? Peppers, potatoes, tomatoes—it takes a lot of time and effort; why would you be making something like that, if you were packing-up your suitcase, in a huff?"

Thinking for a moment, Doyle offered, "Mayhap she was worried about violence, and was trying to sweeten him up, before she broke the news?"

The two detectives looked at each other, knowing neither one of them bought this theory.

"And it seems a bit strange," Doyle observed, "that she hasn't a phone."

"I can't get past the suitcase," Munoz added.

Doyle glanced at her. "What about the suitcase?"

"It's her flat," the other detective pointed out. "Why is she packing-up to leave? She should just change the locks."

Lifting her brows, Doyle said, "Now, there's a very good point."

Munoz continued, "And if we can presume she was scared enough to bug-out, even though it's her own place, then she wouldn't have told him that she was leaving at all—she'd have just left."

"Aye," Doyle agreed. "It doesn't make sense—that she's packin' up, whilst choppin' vegetables. And note that she'd a choppin' knife, close at hand. She was facin' him when she was shot—there must have been a confrontation, and she'd a potential weapon. Why didn't she do somethin' with it?"

"Let's tell Williams."

But after voicing their concerns to their SIO, Williams remained skeptical, mainly because Williams was male, and didn't think any of this was significant, in light of the physical evidence. "That's a little flimsy—and what would be the theory? A third-party staged the murders? Unlikely, with the reported domestic dispute on record. Let's take a canvass of the neighbors, and see what they have to say. The female neighbor on the right, as you face the door, is the one who reported the dispute."

Doyle asked Munoz, "D'you want to take her? I can start on the other end of the hall."

But Williams tilted his head in apology. "I'm not to leave you to your own devices, Sergeant."

This was, no doubt, on Acton's strict orders, and so Doyle conceded, "Yes, sir; I'll tag along with Munoz."

To Munoz, Williams said, "Doyle needs to stay on the floor, please. If you want to go elsewhere, you're to leave her with me."

"Yes, sir."

Williams ducked back into the flat, whilst Munoz knocked on the next-door-neighbor's door. "Police. Open up, please."

There was no immediate response, which was not a surprise; if she'd been home, she'd have come out by now to see what all the fuss was about. Doyle asked, "Did this neighbor call-in the murders, too?"

"No; instead the female victim didn't show up for work, this morning."

Doyle frowned. "So; no one here heard the gunshots? It was early evenin'; you'd think that would set off some alarms, after the reports of a loud quarrel."

Munoz offered fairly, "The weapon was a twenty-two, so it wouldn't be hugely loud. If it was dinner-time, the neighbors might have thought it was a dropped pan, or something."

Since there was no response at the neighboring flat, they walked toward the next.

Munoz said, "I think we should talk to the female victim's employer. They got worried pretty fast, when she went AWOL —didn't even wait a day. Maybe they knew she was in danger."

"Aye—good idea."

They made their way toward the end of the hall, with the majority of residents not answering the door. Since it was mid-day in this working-class neighborhood, this was to be expected, along with the unfortunate fact that sometimes, when neighbors saw police making a canvass, they ducked-out on having to get involved, being as they didn't want to be on the record for anything. The detectives would instead have to wait a few days, and see if anyone felt guilty enough to call the tip-line.

They stood together in the dim hallway, waiting for Williams to finish-up with the Coroner's people. Munoz asked, "Do you mind if I rub your belly, for luck?"

Doyle smiled. "Be my guest."

The other girl ran a hand over Doyle's mounding belly. "This part is hard—feels like his back."

"Aye. The doctor says he's ready to launch." She paused, and then ventured, "How are things goin'?"

Munoz withdrew her hand, and replied, "We went to see a

fertility specialist, but she didn't find anything wrong, and she said at my age, there's no reason to be concerned for at least another year, or so." She made a face. "Mainly, she seemed to think I should just relax, and stop worrying about it."

"Did she indeed?" asked Doyle with interest. "Did you knock her down, Munoz?"

Munoz smiled. "No; Geary was there, so I had to behave myself." She paused. "It's ironic; you worry so much about accidentally getting pregnant, and then it turns out its not as easy as you've been led to believe."

Doyle nodded sympathetically, but made no comment, in that she seemed to fall pregnant whenever Acton happened to glance her way.

The other girl continued, "Geary's not worried; he's humoring me, mainly—but I know he wants children, and the more it doesn't seem to be working, the more I can't help worrying."

"Whist, Munoz; he has the right of it. And now that you know there's nothin' wrong, you'll just need a bit of patience."

"That's what he says. And he says we should enjoy this time, when it's just the two of us."

"Now, there's a good thought. Are you goin' to visit his relatives in Ireland, anytime soon? Lots of people fallin' pregnant, in Ireland."

Munoz smiled, as Doyle had intended. "At Easter, we think. We visited my side during the holidays, and so it's his side's turn for a visit. Which reminds me, there was some woman from the Irish Embassy, who claimed she'd met him in Dublin, but he didn't remember her, so he was suspicious. She said she knew you."

"Probably a bill collector," Doyle joked, but made a mental

note to mention this to Acton, since no doubt it was Aunty Wickham, nosing around. "Don't tell her my 'last known'."

"He's not one to gossip, so you're safe." Dryly, Munoz added, "And you haven't paid a bill since you married Acton."

"There is that," Doyle agreed, and then they straightened up, as Williams came through the flat's door.

CHAPTER 8

"*I*'m inclined to close the case," Williams said, once he and Doyle were back in the car, and headed to headquarters. "We can always re-open, but it seems a clear case of graveyard-love."

Her brows drawn, Doyle replied thoughtfully, "I'd like to interview her employer, before you close it." Belatedly, she added, "Sir."

"I'd have to go with you," he reminded her heavily.

"Just an hour," she wheedled. "We couldn't get any neighbors to go on record, but mayhap the people she worked with will talk. I just don't think this sort of thing happens out of the blue, without the people around her knowin' there was a problem. Usually the neighbors can't wait to give us chapter-and-verse, but here, we've only the one, anonymous complaint."

"Along with the evidence, at the crime scene," he reminded her. "And sometimes, it does just happen out of the blue; he may have had a mental break, or he's so ashamed of something that he made sure she'd never find out."

"Aye," she admitted fairly. "People do strange things, when they're mullycrushed, and panicked—we've seen it, plenty of times."

He glanced over at her. "And besides, the only other option is there's a third-party who set this up, and that doesn't seem likely, to me—that these kind of people would have that kind of enemy."

"Aye," she admitted again. "It doesn't. Although we should find out what he transported—he may have had a target, on his back."

"Then why kill her, too?"

Mulling it over, she conceded, "You're right; it does seem to be a clear case of graveyard-love. I only wish we'd more confirmation that they were quarrelin', and that he was violent. It seems unlikely that a transport company would keep a man who tended to violence, and was licensed to carry."

But he only shrugged a shoulder. "People don't like going on record, Kath—especially if they have to admit they were aware of domestic abuse, but didn't report it."

She sighed. "Right again, DI Williams. Faith, when you think about it, it's a crackin' amazement that anyone comes forward a'tall."

"Very true. We're lucky that some do."

Thinking about this, Doyle was reminded of her friend Dr. Okafor, and added, "You know who's always willin' to come forward? People of faith, who have a clear sense of right-and-wrong, and who aren't afraid to risk themselves."

In a teasing tone, he offered, "Are you talking about Acton? Because Acton has a very clear sense of right-and-wrong."

She made a face. "Touché—but his groundin' principles aren't exactly the same as those of people of faith." She glanced over at him. "Neither are yours, for that matter."

But Williams didn't like to discuss his questionable dealings in the pursuit of Acton-justice, and today was no exception, as he promptly changed the subject. "And that's another landmine; we're trying to decide whether to have Connor baptized. Apparently, Acton has been leaning on Lizzie."

She laughed aloud. "And that, my friend, is my own influence. How gratifyin', that I'm pullin' your strings, in a roundabout way."

He smiled in acknowledgment. "No question that you've been a huge influence on Acton."

She caught a nuance to his tone, and offered, "You're not always certain it's for the better, though."

They drove in silence, for a few beats, and she could see that he debated what to answer. "It depends on your definition of 'better' I suppose. I'll admit that he's in a much better place, on a personal level."

"Well, be warned; I'm workin' on the professional level, too, my friend, and I will point out that you're no help, with all your aidin' and abettin'—you, and Lizzie, too."

He smiled, slightly. "No one 'aids or abets' Acton, and I think that's why he is so good at what he does. He does nothing lightly; he knows when to be patient, and when to back down altogether. I'm not there, yet—I may never be."

"Don't sell yourself short," she teased. "I'm the one who rushes in where angels fear to tread, whilst you're all 'let's close the case in time for tea'."

He leaned his head toward her, as he drove, and explained,

"I meant that I'm more emotional about things, I suppose. It bothers me, when people get away with—with terrible crimes."

"It bothers every one of us, Thomas, but if you believe there is an ultimate justice, then it doesn't rankle, quite so much, because you trust God to get it right." Fairly, she admitted, "You still get bothered though—so much seems *so* unfair—but we can't see the big picture, and the big picture is necessarily very complicated."

He smiled, slightly. "We are back to the baptism topic, I see."

"You must do what you and Lizzie think best, my friend—you're a stubborn boyo, after all. Which makes me wonder; how did that first conversation go, between you and Acton, about your dodgy uncle? 'By the way, I'm thinkin' about committin' a class-one homicide; would you like to lend a hand?'"

But it seemed clear that Williams had decided he'd said too much already, and so he turned the question. "You may as well ask the suspects in the Public Accounts case how that happens, Kath. Someone had to start recruiting the members—who are on a watchdog committee, no less—to see if they were willing to embezzle the money they were supposed to be watching over."

"Aye—boggles the mind, it does. Greed, I suppose. All that lovely money, washin' about, with no one in the bureaucracy payin' very close attention."

He nodded. "Money's always the motivator, it seems. Or most always, anyway—sometimes it's love."

But she shook her head. "No; people don't kill each other over love-love, Thomas; it's thwarted-love, instead. I had this conversation with Officer Gabriel, once—love is not love that seeks its own ends. Instead, it's a mean, selfish sort of love—more like self-love."

He glanced at her. "Like today's case. Graveyard-love."

She quirked her mouth. "I can be stubborn, too, my friend. The jury is still out, on today's case."

He lifted a shoulder in concession. "All right; we'll do a bit more probing, as long as we stay within budget. You have good instincts, Kath—I'll give you that."

"I think it's a female thing; Munoz didn't like the set-up, either."

"Right. I'll send Munoz to talk to her employer, and you and I will talk to his. We should also interview the tip-line people, and see if we can get more information about the neighbor who called-in the argument. But I don't want to allocate more than a couple of hours." He checked the time. "When's your walk-in?"

"Faith, I'm glad you reminded me—there's nothin' like pregnant-brain, to make you forget whether you're afoot or horseback. She'll be there at any minute."

"All right; text me when it's over, and then we'll head over to speak to Mallory, at the tip-line." Touching his screen, he raised Munoz, and asked her to stop by the female victim's employer, to interview whoever was willing.

He then dropped Doyle out front—so that she wouldn't be late for her interview—and she hoisted her rucksack with an air of resignation. "Wish me luck."

"Want me to text, to give you a reason to leave, if it goes too long?"

"No, I can just say that I'm in labor—it's a ready excuse."

With a smile, he pulled away.

CHAPTER 9

*a*s Doyle headed toward the interview room, Acton pinged her, and she lifted the mobile. "Ho."

"I thought I'd check-in."

"My eye is still bloodshot," she advised. Acton was overly-worried about how the corner of her eye always seemed to get bloodshot, in the latter stages of pregnancy.

"A shame; such a lovely eye."

"I notice you avoid makin' mention of my fat feet."

"You malign me; I am very fond of your feet."

She smiled into the phone, because this was undeniably true; Acton liked to cradle her feet in his lap. "Well, I'm attached to them, myself. What are you into, today?"

"I am overseeing a joint task-force meeting."

"Right; I'd forgot. Sounds hideous."

"A necessary evil, I am afraid. I called to remind you about your appointment, this afternoon."

Doyle closed her eyes briefly, as she walked along. "Faith,

I'd forgot—can we push Dr. Easton back? I have a walk-in, and then Williams and I were goin' to do a bit of follow-up, on the graveyard-love case."

"He can bring along another sergeant, perhaps."

She lowered her voice. "I'd like to go, Michael—I've one of my feelin's, I do."

Since Acton knew everything there was to know about her 'feelings', he did not demur any further. "By all means, then. I will see if I can push your appointment back."

"Beg them on bended knee," she teased. There was little doubt that Lord Acton could bring his wife in at midnight, if he so chose. "Got to go; cheers."

Doyle rang off, and pushed open the door to the interview room, where a heavy-set, Hispanic woman was seated at the battered table. As she greeted the witness, Doyle had to refrain from wincing; waves of grief and misery were emanating from the woman, and she bore the same shell-shocked demeanor as did poor Mary.

It was one of the drawbacks of being involved in homicide cases; Doyle tended to deal with grief-stricken people on a daily basis, and being buffeted by strong emotion was always difficult, for someone like her. As a defense mechanism, she always tried to be as business-like as possible, when speaking with the kinfolk who—through no fault of their own—were left to pick up the pieces of their shattered family.

"Officer Doyle," the woman said in greeting, as she mustered up a small smile. "I hope you won't think I'm crazy."

Silently, Doyle withheld her judgement, and smiled politely in return, as she seated herself. "How can I help you today, ma'am?"

In this sort of situation, Doyle tended to make a quick

assessment, to decide whether vague premonitions or neighbor complaints were going to serve as an excuse to meet one of Scotland Yard's finest. Thus far, however, Doyle didn't have that impression—mainly because the witness was so terribly, terribly sad.

"My Yessenia was killed—murdered, three weeks ago," the woman began, and then paused.

"I am so sorry for your loss," Doyle offered in her best business-like voice, which is what they always trained you to say to the grieving relatives—because truly, what else could be said? A parent's worst nightmare had come true, and the woman's bleakness was understandable, even as it was incomprehensible to any other mother. "Has a suspect been apprehended?"

"Oh—oh, yes; they caught him, and he's already in prison. At least, he's off the streets, now, and won't kill anyone else." She leaned forward. "But that's what I wanted to talk to you about, Officer Doyle. I tried to speak with the lady on the tip-line, but I could tell she was very skeptical of what I had to say."

Oh-oh, thought Doyle. So; this witness has a tale of intrigue that no one's buying—the people who answered the tip-line were experts at separating the wheat from the chaff, so to speak, and their judgement was usually spot-on.

Politely, Doyle prompted, "And what did you wish to tell me, ma'am?"

Her companion drew a long breath. "I'm a Christian woman, Officer Doyle, but I was finding it very hard to forgive this man—this man who did such a terrible thing to my daughter. It grieved me."

There was a still, small pause, as Doyle mentally took off

her brisk-police-officer hat, and set it aside. Softly, she agreed, "Aye. That's the hardest thing of all, I think—to be asked to forgive someone, who's done you a terrible wrong."

The woman nodded. "I read about how you were working at the prison, and trying to bring a light into the darkness, and I thought, I should go to the prison to speak to him—speak to her killer. If I could see his humanity, face-to face, then maybe I could forgive him. Maybe, it would help us both."

There was a small pause, and then, with all sincerity, Doyle said, "I don't know as I could have done it. What did he say?"

The woman took a breath. "He said he was sorry. And then, when I asked why he'd done it, he started telling me about the fight over the drugs, and how she'd cheated him out of his fair share." She met Doyle's gaze in bewilderment. "But that's not how it happened—not at all; my daughter was killed in her flat, by an intruder, and there weren't any drugs involved. I think— I think he was talking about another murder. He seemed mixed-up. And so, I asked him about some details, and I didn't correct him when he was wrong, because I think it's important —something's not right, Officer Doyle. If he didn't kill my Yessenia, why is he in prison for it? And who did?"

Doyle pulled her tablet, and began taking notes. The woman was telling the truth, even though it seemed so very hard to believe. "I'll look into it, ma'am. Do you remember the case-detective's name?"

"Yes, Mr. Geary, it was. I thought he'd done so well—to catch him, so fast. But if he caught the wrong man, then maybe he didn't do as well as I thought."

But Doyle had paused, because there was something here —something very troubling. Geary—Munoz's husband—did first-rate work, and he was not someone who was going to nab the wrong suspect—although to be fair, it seemed that the wrong suspect deserved the sentence, too. With a knit brow, she also remembered that her false Aunty had been priming Geary for information—she'd forgot to tell Acton, naturally; mental note to tell him later today. But surely— Wickham wasn't connected to this strange situation —was she?

Slowly, Doyle asked, "I'm not familiar with the file, ma'am, so bear with me; could it be possible that the prisoner was correct? I know we like to think that our children are perfect, but is there any chance that Yessenia was sellin' drugs— mayhap just to her friends, as a lark?"

The woman blinked in surprise. "Oh, no, Officer Doyle; she was a good girl—she was thinking about becoming a police officer. And it wouldn't make any sense, anyway—she was the one who told the authorities about the tainted batch of medication, at New View Pharmacy. She worked there." She paused, a bit sadly. "She was employee of the year."

Holy Mother, thought Doyle, as she stared at the woman in astonishment; *Holy* Mother—Acton famously didn't believe in coincidences, and it almost beggared belief to think that this whistleblower had wound up neatly murdered, but in the wrong homicide file. It *must* be all tied together; someone killed this poor girl, and then covered their tracks by having another murderer carry the blame—a "shadow-murder," the detectives called it.

Struggling to put her thoughts in order, Doyle tried to decide what to ask, her fingers poised. "Was she havin' any trouble at work, because of her goin' forward? Did anyone threaten her, or try to bribe her to stay quiet?"

"Oh, no, Officer Doyle. The police undercover lady told her, very strictly, not to tell anyone, and so she didn't. Save me, of course—even though she wasn't supposed to."

Suddenly alert, Doyle asked in as neutral a tone as she could muster, "Was the undercover lady Irish, like me?"

The witness drew her brows together doubtfully. "I don't know, ma'am. Yessenia told me her name, though, and she had a French name—'Bonnaire,' or something like that."

There was a small pause. "Charbonneau?" Doyle asked, although she already knew the answer.

The witness' brow cleared. "Oh—yes; that was it."

CHAPTER 10

There was a small silence, whilst Doyle concentrated on typing a few nonsense-notes so as to gather her wits together. Leave it to me, she thought a bit crossly, to be a thousand months pregnant, and stumble onto another flippin' crisis.

Doyle looked up from her pretend note-taking. Do you have Yessenia's phone? I'd like to take a look at it."

"Oh, no—sorry. They took Yessenia's phone for evidence. I wish—I wish I could have it back, just to have some of her snaps." She paused, and bit her lip to control the trembling. "Do you think you could ask them, Officer Doyle?"

"I will," Doyle reassured the woman, trying with little success to tamp down the righteous anger that filled her breast. Seizing on the excuse, she added, "In fact, if anyone asks, that's why you came in, today—you wanted me to pull some strings, and get Yessenia's phone back for you." Leaning forward, Doyle emphasized, "You mustn't tell anyone else what you've told me, about the mixed-up murder. It is very, very important." Improvising, she explained, "There's an investigation into sloppy records-keeping, and a lot of people are going to get the sack. Your evidence will be helpful, but we don't want to tip them off."

"Oh," the witness said, wide-eyed. "I understand."

Doyle then escorted the woman to the Security Desk, so that she could sign out, and said in a formal tone for the personnel at the desk, "Thank you for coming in; I will do my best, but the Evidence Locker people aren't the most responsive, sometimes."

"Thank you, Officer Doyle," the woman replied with a covert, conscious look, and then turned to make her way toward the lobby doors.

Williams approached—he'd been hanging about, waiting for her to finish up—and he glanced at the retreating witness. "What did she want?"

"I'll tell you in a mo', but first I've got to go outside, and phone Acton. Can we walk over to the Deli?"

Williams warned, "You probably can't raise him, Kath; he's in on the Bristol joint task-force meeting, right now."

Something in his voice made her antenna quiver, and she eyed him. "Remind me what that one's about. Gangs?" Bristol, unfortunately, carried off the palm for one of the most corrupt and crime-ridden cities in Britain, mainly because it was on the channel, and the population there had a long and storied history of smuggling illegal goods.

"Contraband, which leads to gangs—it's all interrelated. They're cracking down."

She made a skeptical face. "They're *always* crackin' down."

He tilted his head in concession. "This time they're a bit more serious, perhaps."

Caught by a nuance in his tone, she gave him a sharp glance. "What?"

Blandly, he asked, "What, what?"

She blew out an impatient breath. "Keep your precious secrets, then; I've got too many things to keep track of, just now."

He checked his watch. "In the meantime, we can go speak to the tip-line people about what the tipster said, on the graveyard-love case."

But Doyle shook her head. "Can't we take a quick walk to the Deli, Thomas? I truly need to raise Acton, but I don't want to make it look as though it's connected to my walk-in."

This caught his attention, and he willingly fell into step beside her. "Oh? What's up?"

"Let's get outside first, and I'll tell you."

Once outside, Doyle phoned Acton on his work-line, but was immediately sent to voice-mail. She rang off, and contemplated phoning him on their private line—which he'd answer immediately—but she paused, because she didn't want him to think she was in labor, and truly, there wasn't an emergency; the Charbonneau damage had already been done, with poor Yessenia lying in her grave. Better to be patient, than to take his attention away from the umpteenth attempt to rein-in the blacklegs who always seemed to run amok in Bristol.

She explained to Williams, "He's busy, but he'll see that I phoned, and call back at his first opportunity. Let's go to the Deli, to wait it out."

Teasing her, he asked, "Are you sure you can you walk that far?"

She made a face. "We'll see, I suppose. You're a hardy lad; if I break down, you can carry me on your back."

"I am at your service. I'm curious about all the secrecy, though—can't you tell me?"

They began their walk, and she explained, "Here's the nub of it; I think Charbonneau arranged for a murder."

He lifted his brows in surprise. "Charbonneau, the CI?"

The very same. I've always suspected that she arranged for the murder of a prisoner at Wexton Prison, too—someone who was talkin' a bit too freely about the skimmin' rig. So, I'm not over-surprised that she's done another." She glanced at him. "Who oversees the Confidential Informant Unit?"

But he cautioned, "We have to be careful, Kath, because to be a good CI, the informant has to be able to infiltrate the criminals, and do it without raising any suspicions. Sometimes the Met has to look the other way, to preserve the asset."

Annoyed, she retorted, "But we're not goin' to look the other way for murder, for heaven's sake, and I think she's racked up at least two, by now."

He tilted his head in concession. "All right; tell me what the witness said."

"Well, the gist of it is that her daughter was murdered, poor thing, but it seemed to her that they'd nabbed the wrong killer —that he'd done an unrelated murder, instead."

With a skeptical shrug, he asked as they walked along, "And how would she know that?"

"She went to the prison to speak to the perpetrator—to try and forgive him."

There was a small pause. "Wow," he said.

"Wow, indeed. But he started describin' a different murder, with completely different facts." She paused, and then glanced around, to make certain there was no one near. "And the clincher is that her daughter seems to have been some sort of whistleblower, in the tainted-medication case."

He walked a few steps in silence. "Wow, again."

She nodded in emphasis. "Aye. It sounded like the daughter's was a shadow-murder—or more properly, a containment-murder, I suppose, so as to contain the tainted-medication scandal. Anyways, you can see why I'm in a fever to speak to Acton; we'd have a major problem on our hands, if a high-level CI is runnin' interference for the blacklegs on the tainted-medication case."

Frowning, Williams bent his head. "But isn't that the wrong case, Kath? What would the tainted-medication case have to do with Charbonneau?"

Much struck, Doyle stopped dead in her tracks. "Oh. Oh, that's right; I'd forgot. I've got pregnant-brain, and it's a massive burden—be glad you'll never suffer from it."

Williams pointed out the obvious. "Charbonneau wouldn't be a CI in the tainted-medication case—that one's regulatory negligence. A criminal CI wouldn't be involved."

But, thinking this over, Doyle slowly offered, "Unless— unless she was, Thomas. Acton doesn't believe in coincidences, remember?"

He didn't reply, and so she resumed her pace toward the Deli, and mused aloud, "A CI gains a kind of immunity, for helpin' the police, and I wouldn't be surprised if such a thing goes to your head, if you're a criminal type, to begin with. What's to stop you from usin' your position to do whatever will benefit you, knowin' that you can always place the blame on other villains, and you'll be believed?"

"Go on," said Williams thoughtfully.

"Charbonneau was involved in the prison drug-smugglin'—fentanyl, it was. She was involved—we know this for a fact—even though we can't seem to prove it. And now, here we've another situation, involvin' fentanyl. What if Yessenia stumbled across proof that there was some kind of connection?"

He nodded, considering this. "And so, Charbonneau eliminated her?"

"Aye. And then blamed someone else—I imagine a CI would have a long list of people she could pin a murder on. She neatly folds her own murder into another one, with no one askin' too many questions."

But her companion disagreed. "It doesn't really work like that, Kath; everyone knows CIs aren't always reliable—they're good for tip, but not necessarily for hard evidence. They can't just put someone away, at will."

This was true, of course, and it gave her pause. "Aye, that; but there *must* be a tie-in, Thomas, and how else can you explain that the victim worked at New View Pharmacy, reported on their misdeeds, and then Charbonneau swoops in, and arranges for her shadow-murder?"

He slowly shook his head, as they approached the Deli's doors. "I just don't see it; the whistleblower knows New View was not following regulatory protocols, and as a result, they sold a tainted batch of over-the-counter meds. Why would that threaten Charbonneau? I can't make that leap—where's the connection?"

But Doyle had suddenly paused, and nearly swayed on her feet, as she was hit with a truly dreadful thought. Oh, no; she thought in deep dismay, as she closed her eyes briefly. *Oh, no—*

Williams' sharp gaze was upon her, as he steadied her with a hand under her arm. "What? What is it?"

Slowly, she observed, "There *is* a connection between the two cases, Thomas. Nigel Howard was one of the victims, in the tainted-medication case, and he was the laboring-oar on the Public Accounts case. He—he was one of the MPs overseein' the Committee, and he was the one who figured out that gobs of money were goin' missin'."

But her companion frowned, as he steered her toward a table. "I think everyone was immediately suspicious about that, Kath—about how Howard's death was a little too convenient— and so it was looked into rather carefully. It was just a bad batch of opioids, though. After all, eight other people died, too."

"Nine," she corrected rather absently, because her trusty instinct was doing the equivalent of beating her about the head and shoulders, so as to pay attention. Holy Mother, she thought, in dawning horror; could it be? Could the blacklegs have panicked, and got rid of Howard? It was almost unbelievable—mainly because Howard's death wasn't going to put a halt to the investigation, in the first place; the wheels were already in motion. To do something so ruthless—not to mention so cruel, and clumsy—almost beggared belief. On the other hand, the villains in this instance were bureaucrats-in-trouble, and therefore cruel-and-clumsy should probably not come as a surprise.

Williams was silent for a few moments. "So," he said. "You think Howard's may have been an ABC murder."

"Mayhap," she replied somberly. This was a term derived from an Agatha Christie story, where a murderer disguised his true target, by including him in the midst of what appeared to be a random series of killings.

She lifted her eyes to meet his. "I'm not sure what to think, but I'm fairly certain that you know more about all this than you're lettin' on."

He lowered his gaze, and contemplated the tabletop in silence.

And there you go, thought Doyle, with a sinking feeling. She'd thought it a little odd, that Williams hadn't immediately asked the identity of the SIO, who'd botched Yessenia's case—it was the first thing she'd wanted to know. She was also reminded that Lizzie had been asking Mary about whether any drugs had been left in the flat, and the combination of these troubling factors inspired her to retort, with a full measure of exasperation, "Keep all your precious secrets, Thomas; if people are gettin' themselves murdered, that's none o' your concern."

Stung, he lifted his gaze, and countered, "Everything's not a simple case of right-and-wrong, Kath—and no one knows this better than you, I might add. You've weighed your choices so as to protect your family, and I've never blamed you. But now I've got a family to protect, too."

Mainly because this was all too true—she was often in a cleft-stick, when it came to her husband—Doyle immediately reached for his hand. "I'm that sorry, Thomas; it's that 'divided loyalties' thing again, and I never seem to learn my lesson. I'm the pot and you're the kettle, and you will do as you think best, which is only right, and just. Please, please forgive me."

Mollified, he disclosed. "I do know that Acton is aware that Charbonneau's a big problem, and he's working on it."

Making a wry mouth, she filled in what he'd left unsaid.

"And it's better all-'round if no one like me blunders in, makin' accusations and tippin' the villains off that they are on Acton's radar. All right, I understand."

He nodded. "He needs to find out exactly who's involved, and so it's at a delicate stage, right now. I think he's being patient, and waiting for certain people to let down their guard, thinking they're in the clear."

She pressed her lips together, thinking of Mary's heartache —and Yessenia's mother's, too. "He's miles more patient than I would be."

"Me, too. That's why he's so much better suited than we are, to decide how to go forward, and achieve the best result."

"Best, in his eyes," she retorted, nettled.

But Williams stood firm. "He knows how to factor everything in, and come up with the 'least-worst' result. I may not always agree, but I tend to trust his judgement."

Doyle decided not to get into yet another argument about whether Acton should be doing-what-he-did in the first place, and so she asked, "Do I let on that you've told me this?"

"Whatever you want," he replied, and met her eyes. "After all, you're only doing what you think best, too."

With a sigh, she declared, "You're a better friend than I, Thomas Williams."

"I don't think it's a contest, Kath."

"Well, speakin' of doin'-whatever-he-thinks-best, here comes the undisputed champion," Doyle noted, as her husband came through the Deli doors, and walked over to join them.

CHAPTER 11

"I can only stay for a moment," Acton told them, as he gave Doyle an assessing glance, and pulled out a chair. "Everything all right?"

"Yes—I'm not in labor," she said immediately. "I'm sorry, if I gave you a start."

Williams rose, and pushed in his chair. "I'll head back, and arrange for the tip-line interview."

"I'll be right there," Doyle assured him, and then said to her husband, "We may as well walk back—I wouldn't want to keep your task-force waitin'."

"A shame," he replied, as he helped her to rise. "And here I was hoping I'd have an excuse to withdraw."

She suggested, as they walked out the door. "I could always claim a bout of false labor, if you're that desperate."

"Don't tempt me."

She took his arm, and they began their rather slow progress back toward headquarters. "How are things, in Bristol?"

"Never-ending," he replied briefly.

She squeezed his arm in sympathy. "'Tis the nature of the beast, I suppose. A channel city, where the citizens tend to have sharp elbows, when it comes to the government tellin' them what to do."

"A very apt description."

"Well, I don't want to add to your burdens, Michael, but I am startin' to think that Howard's was an ABC murder."

He took a couple of strides in silence, and then asked in a mild tone, "What did Williams say?"

"He said nothin', of course, because he'd rather be tortured than give up your secrets. But I'd a witness, this mornin', who told a strange tale, and so I put two and two together, like I tend to do."

"You do, indeed. Tell me about this witness, if you would."

Doyle recited the details from her interview that morning, as her husband listened without comment. At its conclusion, he continued quiet, and so she added, "I know you don't like to tell me classified things, for fear that I'll blunder in, but you have to remember that if you *don't* tell me classified things, I'm just as likely to blunder in, anyways."

"It is a dilemma," he admitted.

"Well, let's have the truth, with no bark on it, Michael; how certain are you that Howard was murdered?"

"I am fairly certain," he replied quietly, and it was the truth.

Although she'd already guessed as much, it was painful to hear it confirmed. "Saints and holy angels," she breathed, and shook her head in utter dismay. "Was it Charbonneau, who was behind it?"

"I would not be surprised if she were involved, yes."

With some alarm, she asked, "Don't you have enough to

send-out an All Ports Warnin', and bring her in, Michael? For heaven's sake; people are bein' murdered—you can't stall the case, so as to arrange your evidence 'just so', if it means more people are goin' to be put into danger."

But he pointed out, in a practical manner, "We have to build a case, Kathleen. We have to make it stick, if we are to keep her off the streets."

Unfortunately, this was oftentimes a detective's dilemma; a suspect could be brought in on a lesser charge immediately, but the investigative team would want to cultivate enough evidence to support a major crime, and thus would hold back, to see what further evidence might develop—sometimes to everyone's all-around regret. It appeared, based on her husband's reply, that this was exactly the situation for the fair Charbonneau—and Doyle could see how it would be a tricky thing; the reason the ABC technique had been used, after all, was because it would be difficult to prove that these murders were deliberate, rather than negligent. Evidence that would support a murder-one charge against Charbonneau would be hard to come by.

Reminded, Doyle said a bit anxiously, "The security tape from my interview should be scrubbed, then—I wouldn't want to put the witness in danger."

"Yes," he agreed, and lifted his mobile to call Williams.

After he rang off, they walked a few more steps in silence, until she ventured, "Well—and I will say it pains me, because this is such an odd reversal of roles—can't you just arrest Charbonneau on *somethin'*? Better that she's in the nick, because who knows what else, she's been behind. Faith, we should probably do a thorough review of all the cases, where she's been the key informant."

But he only tilted his head in mild disagreement. "I'm afraid it is a delicate situation."

Something in his tone made her antenna quiver, and she glanced up in alarm. "Exactly how grim *are* things?"

He covered her hand with his own. "Not as grim as they might appear," he assured her, and it was the truth. "I have a fair concept of how things stand, and I have only to decide the best way forward."

Which was, of course, exactly what Williams had hinted—Acton was trying to decide the "least-worst" resolution, to this tangle-patch. And, if it was a "delicate matter," this might indicate that there was a personal element involved, too; after all, Acton had no delicacy at all, when it came to rolling-up random blacklegs.

Taking a guess as to the personal element, she ventured, "Williams seems to think that he may be in danger—him or Lizzie, mayhap."

He neither confirmed nor denied, but said only, "We must tread very carefully, certainly, lest another murder be provoked."

Somberly, she nodded. "Aye. Because these people aren't clear-thinkers, they're panicked bureaucrats. Faith, you almost wish you were dealing with one of the mafia gangs, since they're professionals, and thus would have the good sense to lie low, whilst the heat is on."

"It is a volatile situation. I would urge you to say nothing of this, Kathleen."

She glanced up at him. "What do I tell my walk-in?"

"If you will give me her information, I will take over from here."

Reminded, Doyle said, "She'd like her daughter's phone

back—it's in the Evidence Locker. And that's our cover story, for her comin' in—I told her not to tell anyone else her tale."

"Good," he agreed. "I will look into the phone."

Oh, thought Doyle, as they walked through the lobby doors. Now, that's a wrinkle; I don't think he's going to look into it, at all.

CHAPTER 12

*A*fter Doyle parted from her husband in the lobby, Williams caught up with her to say that Mallory wasn't available for her scheduled interview.

"The tip-line supervisor isn't sure why she didn't come back from lunch. I'm surprised she didn't show—she's a big fan of yours, remember?"

Doyle made a face. "Faith, it's just as well, Thomas; I don't want any snaps taken of me, just now. Should we go and visit the male victim's employer, instead?"

He checked the time, and decided, "No—I think a transport company usually works early morning to early afternoon, so they're probably closing up. Let's push it off until tomorrow."

"All right, then; on a happy note, Acton didn't say anything about reschedulin' my doctor's appointment, so I can go home with a clear conscience."

"I'll walk you out."

"Like a good watchdog," she teased, as she texted Adrian to

come fetch her. "Truly, there's no need, Thomas; nothin's goin' to befall me, standin' on the pavement in front of headquarters."

But as they passed through the lobby doors, he said in a low tone, "I wanted to ask about what Acton had to say—about your walk-in. He wanted me to lift the surveillance-tape of the interview."

Doyle took a glance around, and lowered her voice. "He basically affirmed what we'd suspicioned, about Howard. But he said he had to step carefully, for fear of sparkin' off even more murders."

He nodded, unsurprised. "I hope I don't have to tell you to be careful, Kath. Acton wanted that tape scrubbed without delay."

She leaned against the wall, with her hands cushioning her lower back. "You know, Thomas, if Charbonneau's a crooked CI, it stands to reason that she'd have access to security, inside the Met—it would only make sense, with what we know. Faith, she may even have cohorts, on the inside."

"And the outside," he added. "I bet that Acton was right, and your fake aunt was sent-out by Charbonneau—it's too much of a coincidence, otherwise. Did Acton say whether he'd managed to identify her?"

"Oh—in all the grim drama about Howard's murder, I forgot to ask if he'd found out anythin' more. We do know her identity, though; she's Georgia Wickham, and she's attached to the Irish Embassy."

He gave a low whistle. "Really?"

"It's a high-level con," she explained with some pride. "Only the best cons will do, for the Doyle family."

But he frowned at bit, thinking over this revelation. "I don't know; sending-in a fake aunt doesn't seem very high-level. It's hard to believe they thought you'd fall for it."

"Aye," she readily agreed. "And even if I did, Acton certainly wouldn't. It's all very strange."

"Be careful; she may not be rational," he warned.

"Oh, she's rational," Doyle replied. "She's just a lyin' liar. Acton thinks the blacklegs on the Public Accounts Commission are tryin' to leverage some immunity, out of this charade."

But Williams was openly skeptical. "That's hard to believe, Kath. Anyone who knows you, knows that you wouldn't be very sympathetic to her claim in the first place."

"True enough," she agreed. "Which only shows you, they didn't look into it very deeply. I'd show my dear Aunty the door, before I'd ever make a pitch to keep her out o' prison."

He was quiet for a few moments, thinking, and then he suggested, "Could there be a different goal, behind it?"

She looked over at him with interest. "What would it be, though, Thomas?"

"Maybe she just wants to get close enough to plant a listening device."

Shaking her head, Doyle replied, "That doesn't seem likely; we met her at Tim's, and she's never made any attempt to come to the flat. Instead, she wants to meet me for tea, somewhere."

He made a derisive sound. "Like you'd drink tea."

She smiled. "Again; it's clear she didn't do her homework."

Oh, she suddenly realized; I forgot to tell Acton that my false Aunty was trying to winkle information from Geary. He'll want to touch-up with him, and find out what she wanted to know. And—come to think of it—it's a bit odd, that my husband didn't quiz me about the wretched Ms. Wickham, on our walk back from the Deli; he didn't ask whether she'd tried to make contact—almost as though he's well-aware that she hasn't.

He's monitoring her, she concluded. And small blame to him—I know he's very unhappy, about my Aunty. But he's trying to hide how unhappy he is, so as not to upset me, because that's his standard operating procedure—to try not to upset me, which oftentimes leads to just the opposite, since I'm one to blunder about, all unknowing.

As they waited, Williams took the opportunity to pull his mobile, and check-in on his son.

After he rang off, Doyle teased, "You can always take paternity leave, you know."

But he sheathed his phone, and shook his head. "There's too much going on, right now."

"Well, I'm soon to be exiled to maternity leave, so don't you dare get together with the fair Mallory, and solve the graveyard-love case without me. Faith, but I hate bein' sidelined."

"You should be happy to rest, for a change," he scolded. "Lizzie said you were at Mary's, this morning."

"I'm just not wired to loll about, Thomas—I'd go barkin' mad. And Lizzie was over there just as early, even though she's worn to a thread."

He bowed his head in concession. "She wants to help out, and it's hard for me to argue."

"Exactly. And d'you know who's been a shinin' star, in all this? Savoie, of all people. He's been helpin' Mary get Gemma to school in the mornings, and then drivin' her over to Mass."

Williams made a skeptical sound, because he didn't much like Savoie, being as the two men had a long and antagonistic history.

Doyle smiled at his reaction, and insisted, "Well, you've got to hand it to him, Thomas; he turned over a leaf, after he adopted Emile, and now he always puts that boyo front and center." Teasing, she added, "You two have a lot in common, now, with your snaps of Connor, and always checkin' in on him."

But Williams replied rather stiffly, "I have a hard time believing that leopard has changed his spots, Kath. Savoie has a long history of criminal conduct."

Fairly, she conceded, "Well, I'm not sayin' he's singin' in the choir, or anythin', but you do find out who your true friends are, in a crisis, and he's proved his mettle—I'll give him that."

"Which reminds me, Lizzie thinks we should go ahead with the baptism, and get it over with." With a palpable lack of enthusiasm, Williams added, "We have to go meet with your priest, tomorrow, and be counseled about it."

"He'll not put any pressure on you, Thomas, don't worry." She paused. "I'd tease you about it, but I know that it must rankle."

He took a breath. "No—it's not a big deal, and I feel as though it's a box that I may as well tick-off. It might be important to Connor, some day."

Doyle couldn't resist a smile. "You see? You and Savoie are like peas in a pod. You should meet-up for lunch, and compare parentin' notes."

"Not funny, Kath," he replied heavily.

CHAPTER 13

*O*nce home, Doyle greeted the exuberant Edward with not-quite-so-equal exuberance, and then bundled him off for a trip to the playground, in the park across the street—their usual routine, on the days she worked. The boy needed to run off some energy after his nap, and—as Doyle was supposed to be engaging in mild exercise, herself—a trip to the playground served the purpose, being about as far as she could travel, nowadays, without needing to stop and rest.

And it was no hardship, for her. She very much enjoyed her work, but she very much enjoyed the visits to the playground, too—even though the two worlds could hardly be more different. She'd be caught-up in crime-scenes, and deadlines, and lab reports, and then—suddenly—her life would slow down immensely, with the only task being the rather tedious business of teaching little children how to play nicely—that, and the constant battle to shake the sand from their shoes.

Any such outing necessarily included Reynolds and

Trenton, their security-man, but Doyle had grown accustomed, because she couldn't blame Acton; her due-date was fast approaching, and there were false relatives, climbing out of the woodwork.

As they walked across the street, Reynolds inquired, "And how was Miss Mary today, madam?"

"I think she's findin' her feet, a bit. She's counselin' with Father John every mornin', and believe me, there's no one better, to pull one through a crisis."

"I am happy to hear it, madam. Such a tragedy."

"It's almost lucky that she's got herself a newborn, to keep her occupied. Although the poor wee lass will never know her father."

Reynolds clucked in dismay. "A terrible shame, madam. We can hope Miss Mary will re-marry, perhaps."

Doyle tried to decide if Reynolds was hinting that he'd be willing to take-up that particular mantle, but decided she didn't get that impression—Reynolds seemed devoted to bachelorhood, and to the House of Acton; it was hard to imagine the man pledging his allegiance to a wife. Mayhap— mayhap Mary would wind-up with Tim McGonigal; Melinda Clarence had once said they were both 'plain vanilla', and they did seem rather well-suited. Although she truly shouldn't be matching-up poor Mary up with anyone, just now.

As they turned onto the path toward the playground, Edward ran ahead in happy anticipation, and Doyle asked Reynolds, "How was the boyo, today? Did he run you ragged?" Doyle had duly noted that Callie was absent, yet again, but didn't want to bring it up with Reynolds, since Reynolds tended to be over-impatient with the young nanny.

"Not at all, madam; his energy needs only to be channeled.

Although I have discovered that he thoroughly enjoys disrupting my telephone conversations."

Doyle laughed. "Join the club—it's enough to make you lock 'im in the lift."

"Indeed. Lady Madeline phoned, and wished to speak with Lord Acton. I'm afraid I could barely hear her, above the din."

Doyle knit her brow. "Remind me who Lady Madeline is, Reynolds."

"The late Father Clarence's mother, madam."

"Oh—oh, that's right; she's from up north, somewhere. Faith, what did she want?"

"She was rather insistent, actually." This, said in a tone of mild disapproval, because Reynolds was very certain of the pecking-order, betwixt a belted Earl and a mere Baroness from Yorkshire. "She asked for Lord Acton's personal mobile phone number, but I explained that I was not at liberty to disclose such information."

Doyle blew out a breath. "Definitely not. Acton's got his hands full, and doesn't need to be speakin' with elderly ladies who want to bend his ear. How did she get our phone number at the flat, in the first place?

"I believe Melinda Clarence may have given it to her."

"Oh—I imagine you are right. I suppose I should sympathize more; poor Lady Madeline has lost her son—not to mention she's gained a surprise daughter-in-law, which must have been a massive shock, being as her son was a priest, and had no business gettin' married, in the first place. We shouldn't be annoyed, that the woman's a bit bewildered, and wants to pose a few questions."

"Indeed, madam."

Suddenly struck, Doyle warned, "Although she may be

tryin' to glom-on, instead. She'd better not be askin' Acton for money, since we both know she'll catch cold at that."

"Unlikely, madam; I believe the Clarence family is quite wealthy."

"Are they? Well then, that's one less worry. I hope she won't be a pest, though; the last thing our Callie needs is a step-gran, seekin' out her attention. She's had a lot to sort-out, lately."

Reynolds met this mention with stony silence, being as he did not approve of Callie's absences-without-leave, particularly since Edward was best handled by a tag-team.

Mentally castigating herself for forgetting that she shouldn't mention Callie, Doyle swiftly added, "Once I'm on maternity leave, I'll be on Edward-watch, and your burden will be miles lighter, my friend."

"Not at all, madam; I quite enjoy my time with Master Edward."

She smiled, "As long as you stay off the phone, and hide his copy of *The Gingerbread Man*."

The butler offered a slight smile. "He does enjoy the story, madam."

"Well, it's all a bit ironic, because Acton's got his own version of a gingerbread woman," she observed. "This one's got immunity, of sorts, and so he can't seem to catch her."

"Who is this, madam?"

Belatedly reminded that she probably shouldn't be bleating out state secrets, Doyle nonetheless realized that Reynold might have some helpful information. When they'd had their kerfuffle at Wexton Prison, it seemed clear that Reynolds was already acquainted with Charbonneau—which was quite the surprise to the fair Doyle, as it was hard to imagine how the impeccably correct butler would be rubbing shoulders with a criminal CI.

Vaguely, she answered, "Just for a case, he's workin' on. The good guys need evidence and such, to lock-up the blacklegs, and sometimes it's truly frustratin'."

"A necessary evil, madam, but the justice system must be respected."

"Right," she said a bit hastily, since it was undeniable that the master of the house didn't care two pins about respecting the justice system. "But—speakin' of blacklegs—remember when we went on our field-trip, to Wexton Prison? Plenty of blacklegs, there—some were incarcerated, and some were runnin' the place. Such a day, that was."

Delicately, Reynolds shuddered. "I'll not soon forget, madam."

"Well, all's well that ends well, I suppose—save for Martina Betancourt, God rest her soul. Although she was a lot like Charbonneau, when she was servin' her time at Wexton. They were both fish-out-of-water; far too posh, to be minglin' with the prisoners in the general population."

As though suddenly remembering, Doyle turned to him. "She'd already met you, hadn't she? When we saw Charbonneau at the prison, she was that gobsmacked, to behold you, standin' there."

A bit stiffly, Reynolds replied, "A chance acquaintance, only, madam. I do not normally interact with criminals."

Doyle persisted, "What sort of 'chance acquaintance', my friend? Never say you met at the gym, or somethin'?"

To her surprise, she could see that Reynolds was experiencing no little inner turmoil, in trying to determine how to respond. Oh-ho, she thought with great interest; now we're getting somewhere—I've struck a nerve, all unknowing.

"Ms. Charbonneau was the acquaintance of an acquaintance," the butler carefully explained. "I did not know her personally."

This, interestingly enough, was true, but was said in such a repressive tone that Doyle felt she could pry no more—or not at the moment, at least. As they made their way through the playground's wrought-iron gates, she thought this over, and decided that Acton must have set-up Reynolds in some situation, so as to garner information from Charbonneau—that was the only explanation that made sense, and would also explain Reynolds' reluctance to unbutton his lip.

With a small, inner sigh, she acknowledged to herself that she needed to follow-up on this strange circumstance, because it was important, for some reason. It was important that the fair Doyle discover how Reynolds had met Charbonneau— although exactly *why* this was important wasn't at all clear.

Willingly, she allowed Reynolds to change the subject, and walked along as though she'd nothing more pressing on her mind save the options he presented for the dinner menu, that night.

CHAPTER 14

emma and Emile were already at the playground, being as they usually came straight over from St. Margaret's, with the school being within easy walking distance.

Emile's father, Philippe Savoie, was also at his usual post, standing at the perimeter, and keeping a sharp eye on his son. The boy was a bit older than the others, and had to be monitored, because oftentimes he'd attempt something reckless, which would then prompt the littler children to try and emulate him, with disastrous results.

Doyle had to hand it to Savoie—the other fathers would often use the outing as an excuse to sit on a bench and review their phones, but he always stood vigilant, cautioning Emile on occasion, and lending a hand whenever Gemma needed a boost to the monkey-bars.

Gemma was Mary's adopted daughter, and—ever since Howard's tragic death—Savoie regularly brought her along with Emile, when they came from the school over to the park. It was yet another kindness, since Gemma and Emile were fast-friends, and enjoyed playing together.

Little Edward enjoyed playing with them, too, even though he wasn't quite old enough to be a fast-friend. In the time-honored manner of smaller children, he doggedly wanted to join the other two whenever possible, and strongly objected to being left out.

Doyle watched Gemma laugh and play, and decided that the little girl didn't seem to be overly shaken-up, by her stepfather's death. She was still so young, and in any event, children tended to look forward, rather than backward.

Savoie willingly stepped forward to rescue Gemma, when the girl found herself stranded on the climbing wall, and—although she was longing for a sit-down on the bench, after her long day—Doyle decided that she should assist him in his duties, and so she walked over to stand beside him.

"Hallo, Philippe; how nice to see you, when there's no one shootin' at us."

But Savoie was not interested in waxing nostalgic, and instead asked, in his abrupt way, "*Bien.* I must ask the question."

"Ask away."

"*Le bébé*, she breathes, *parfois*, like this." He demonstrated, by catching his breath in small gasps. "Not always," he explained; "but sometimes."

"Oh. I think that's normal, in little babies, whilst they're figurin' out how everythin' works. Edward used to do the same thing, and after about the twentieth time, your heart doesn't stop."

Savoie's nodded. *"Bien.* I do not know *les bébés.* Emile, he was not the baby, for me."

"Oh—that's right, you got him when he was already fully-operational. Well it's a steep learnin' curve, my friend."

He bent his head, to confide, "I ask you, because I did not wish to make the worry, for Marie."

"And good on you, Philippe; Mary has enough worries, as it is."

They stood for a moment, watching the shrieking children, with Doyle hiding her bemusement that Savoie—of all people —had apparently added Mary's baby to the list of things he bothered about. It was so unexpected—Savoie was an unrepentant bachelor, after all—but then again, the Frenchman had felt the same way about Emile, when the little boy had been a loose-end child.

It was something psychological—Dr. Harding had said something, once, about Savoie. The psychiatrist had said that he was transferring something about something—she couldn't really remember, but it seemed clear that some kind of chord was struck, whenever Savoie came across a child in need— probably because it reminded him of himself, when he was little.

In all sincerity, she offered, "Mary says you've been a mighty boon, Philippe, and well done, you. Poor thing—she's had a rough road, not to mention that she's been through this before, with her first husband. It hardly seems fair."

But Savoie wasn't interested in sympathy-talk, and instead said, "I must ask another of the questions."

Hiding her amusement, Doyle nodded. "Right then; I'm ready."

"Gemma, I help her with *les devoirs*—the school-work, at

home. She and Emile, they do this work *après-midi*—in the afternoon, while Marie sleeps."

"Oh—I see," said Doyle, trying to keep up.

He made an impatient sound. "There is much of the *Anglais*, in this school-work, and I do not know the *Anglais*, very well."

She smiled. "You're askin' the wrong person for help, you know, but I'll be happy to pitch in."

He frowned impatiently. "*Non, non*; you must rest, little bird. It is Monsieur Reynolds, who could do the helping. Do you think he would do this?"

Doyle lifted her brows. "I suppose we could ask, but the poor man's bein' run ragged, lately."

"I will pay him—*très généreux*," Savoie assured her.

Feeling a bit ashamed that she couldn't hold a candle to Savoie's efforts to aid the grieving widow, Doyle offered, "Mayhap we could arrange for it, whilst Edward takes his nap —as long as they're quiet—but let me be the one to ask Reynolds, Philippe, so that he knows he can say 'no', if he wants to."

"*Bien*," said Savoie, with the satisfied air of someone who knows exactly what the servant's answer will be.

Oh, thought Doyle, oh—that's right; Reynolds owes Savoie for a spot of murder, that the two of them hatched-up.

In an almost unbelievable turn of events, Reynolds had enlisted Savoie to kill Gemma's nemesis; a Russian Colonel, who held the power to take Mary's little girl back to Russia, and use her as a pawn in his questionable political plans.

It was all rather amazing—that the unassuming butler had participated in a murder-plot—but it was one of those "shades of grey" situations that Williams didn't think Doyle could appreciate, even though she could. Gemma had never been formally adopted by Mary and her husband—her first husband, that was. Instead, they'd been laying low, and trying to hide the little girl from the Russian faction that saw her as a means to power—Gemma was related to Russian royalty, or some such; Doyle forgot exactly how.

But fate then stepped in, and Gemma's true identity was exposed, with Mary having no legal right to keep her daughter, who she loved with her whole heart.

It was all very complicated—being as there were international ramifications—but Acton would have been powerless to stop the Colonel's plans, which included a child-marriage, so as to gain authority over the girl. And so, Reynolds had steeled himself to do what he thought was necessary, so as put a stop to it, himself.

Doyle considered this extraordinary episode with all the wonder it deserved, and thought—now, there's another conversation that it would be hard to imagine; Reynolds, initiating a conversation with Savoie on the hunch that he was someone who was well-able to commit a discreet little murder. Not to mention how handy it must have been, to have a seasoned criminal in one's circle of acquaintances.

But mayhap, it wasn't so hard to imagine, after all; Savoie's son was very attached to Gemma—as they all were—not to mention that if the little girl had indeed been spirited back to Russia, it would have broken poor Mary's heart. On top of the all the other heartbreaks, of course—small wonder, that Acton had decided the Colonel's murder investigation should go cold.

And—although Doyle was naturally uneasy about this shocking little episode—she was also willing to leave well-enough alone. With a mental sigh, she admitted to herself that everything was miles more complicated than it used to be, before she'd married Acton. Or mayhap it was always this complicated, but she'd been blissfully unaware, and happily living in her right-is-right, and wrong-is-wrong little world.

And so, Savoie had now maneuvered her into asking Reynolds for this homework favor—which he'd agree to, of course; they all wanted to ease Mary's burdens—even though Doyle held a strong suspicion that the master of the house wouldn't be best pleased with such an arrangement. Acton wasn't as much worried about grieving widows as he was worried about his pregnant wife's peace of mind, and so she'd have to do a bit of wheedling.

Doyle excelled at wheedling her husband, of course, but nonetheless, she decided that she should fortify herself for the task ahead. "I'll take Reynolds over to the kiosk for coffee, and buttonhole him along the way. Can I bring you a cup?"

But Savoie only shook his head. "*Non*. If I drink the coffee, I will want the cigarette."

Doyle blinked in surprise. "Never say you're givin' up smokin'?"

"*Oui*. He indicated his shoulder with a grimace. I have *le patch à fumer*."

In some bemusement, she exclaimed, "Mother a' Mercy, Philippe; next thing, you and Acton will be swappin' kale recipes."

"*Pardon*?

"Never you mind; let me round-up Reynolds, and ask your favor."

"*Bien*," the Frenchman replied, and then turned back to the children, with a satisfied air.

CHAPTER 15

*a*s expected, Reynolds readily agreed to the homework-plan, and Doyle could discern no masked dismay, at the proposal.

"I don't want you to be resentful, and quit on us, Reynolds," she cautioned. You may snub wretched Savoie with my whole-hearted blessin'."

"Not at all, madam—if we can manage it while Master Edward is napping, it will be no trouble at all."

"Aye; we can't let Edward know that the others are upstairs, else he'll get a grapplin' hook, and scale the walls." Taking a casual sip, she advised, "Let me mention it to Acton before you do, though."

"Certainly, madam. Only let me know when we will start the sessions, so that I may prepare the materials needed."

To Doyle's surprise, when they returned to the playground, it was to see that Callie had arrived, and was holding-up Edward by the waist, as he navigated the monkey-bars, whilst Savoie and Trenton each stood at a distance, and watched the proceedings. The young nanny glanced over at Doyle and Reynolds, and lifted her fingers in a greeting. She looked a bit self-conscious, though, as well she should.

Cheerily, Doyle waved back, "Ho, Callie." Under her breath to Reynolds, she warned, "Be nice."

"Certainly, madam," he replied, and then called out, "How very good it is to see you again, Miss Callie."

Since this was said in what might be considered an equivocal tone, Doyle hastily approached the girl, and offered, "Faith, if I'd known you were comin', I'd have got you some coffee, too."

"I'm sorry that I haven't been in touch," the young nanny replied in a constrained tone. "I haven't been feeling well."

This was not true, but Doyle waved her cup. "No worries, Callie, we're that happy you're feelin' better."

"Watch me, Miss Callie," Emile called out, from his perch atop the climbing wall.

"Emile," warned Savoie.

Trenton had moved to the perimeter of the playground, where he now stood at a small distance from Savoie—which was only to be expected. Trenton didn't much like Savoie, and he was always careful to maintain a "ready" position, when the Frenchman was about.

For his part, Savoie roundly ignored Trenton, although he seemed to do it with a faint air of amusement, which Doyle felt only tended to exacerbate the situation.

I am longing for the day, she admitted to herself, when I can just walk over to the park without bringing an entourage, and getting myself caught-up in all the crackin' cross-currents.

Mayhap the playground is more like the Met than it would appear, at first blush.

Out of the corner of her eye, Doyle saw Trenton signal to Reynolds, and almost immediately, the butler suggested that Doyle retreat to sit on a bench. "You must rest, madam."

"Aye, then," Doyle replied easily, because she was outnumbered, and wasn't much use for lifting small boys, in the first place. "Come sit with me for a mo', Callie, and we'll catch up."

The girl willingly relinquished her post to Reynolds, and then accompanied Doyle to settle-in on a nearby bench. "How are you feeling, Lady Acton?"

"I'm ready for it all to be over, and to see my feet again—I've missed them."

Callie smiled a bit wanly. "I can't wait to meet the new baby."

"Your nephew," Doyle noted. "Now, isn't that a corker? Little did we know."

"Definitely," the girl replied, and attempted a smile.

Faith, she's a bundle of misery, thought Doyle. Poor lass.

"How's our Melinda?" Doyle asked, as she took a casual sip. "Is she drivin' you mad?" Melinda Clarence had been recently revealed as Callie's birth mother.

Again, the girl attempted a smile. "No—no, she's just—she's just a bit—"

"Drivin' you mad," Doyle filled in, with her own smile.

Callie offered, "She means well, of course. She keeps telling me that I'll have plenty of money, once her late husband's estate settles."

Doyle weighed whether to discuss the late Father Clarence, and decided it would be best to avoid that particular tangle-patch. "Well, a bit of dosh is always welcome, I suppose."

Callie made a face. "She's hinting that I should move-in with her."

"And you don't want that?"

Doyle could discern a wave of sadness, as her companion pressed her lips together. "No, that wasn't—it wasn't in my plans."

Doyle was reminded that Callie had suffered a recent disappointment in her love-life, according to Adrian, and so she said a bit briskly, "Just tell Melinda 'no,' then, Callie—may as well start as you mean to go on. And recall that she's probably dealin' with guilt, along with everythin' else, and is doin' that 'over-compensate' thing that the psychiatrists always bang on about."

The girl nodded. "Yes, I'm sure you're right."

They paused, because a heated dispute had broken out amongst several older children about whose turn it was at the climbing-wall, and Savoie promptly walked over to extract Emile, and put him in time-out on a bench.

Watching this, Doyle remarked with some amusement, "Glad he's not my da; he runs a tight ship."

"Yes," said Callie in a constrained tone. "He's a good father."

Doyle caught a jolt of misery, and offered, "Your da is a good father too, lass—he's the one who opened his heart to you, and loved you, all these years. And he's your true da, no matter what the genetics say."

"Yes, I know," she agreed, but the girl's gaze strayed back to Savoie, who was busy giving Emile a talking-to.

Thinking to change the subject, Doyle asked, "Now that

you're feelin' better, can you come over for dinner? Acton needs to get accustomed to havin' a decent relative, underfoot."

Wanly, the girl smiled again. "I saw Lord Acton yesterday, as a matter of fact. He'd asked if I could come his office, at the Met."

Doyle blinked. "Did he?"

Callie nodded. "He wanted to warn me about Dr. Tim's new girlfriend. She'd gone to tea with me—she's trying to get acquainted with his friends and family." She paused, and pressed her lips together. "Lord Acton thinks she may be a gold-digger, though. He warned that I should stay away, and that I shouldn't give her any information."

"Oh," said Doyle, thoroughly dismayed. "Yes, I think he's heard that she's a bit dodgy—we didn't think to warn you."

A bit defiantly, the girl offered, "I was surprised he said it— she seemed so nice. In fact, she asked a lot of questions about you; she'd read about you in the news, I think."

Lightly, Doyle made to turn the subject. "If you are ever tempted to jump off a bridge, Callie, my advice is to just keep walkin'."

But Callie had not been distracted, and asked with some concern, "Does Dr. Tim know that she may be a problem?"

"He does now, poor man. Mother a' Mercy, but he has the worst luck."

"We both do," said Callie, with an air of unhappiness. "We should start a club."

But Doyle wasn't having it, and mock-scolded, "Whist, a winsome girl like you has got to be brushin' the boys away, like so many flies. Enough of this, or I'll think you're fishin' for compliments."

Callie mustered up a smile. "All right, Lady Acton."

"Kathleen," Doyle corrected. "We're sisters, now—although neither one of us has the least notion of how that works."

"Kathleen," Callie repeated, but she seemed distracted, as her eyes strayed to Emile, when the boy returned to the playground.

CHAPTER 16

They'd already crossed the street and were heading toward home, when they spied Acton, walking to meet them.

"Da!" shrieked Edward, and ran pell-mell to his father. Acton swung him up without breaking stride, as the little boy then clung to his neck, hooting with delight.

Oh-oh; my husband's all on-end, thought Doyle, as she smiled and kissed him in greeting. "You're home early," she said, and waited with some apprehension.

She was to be given no dire news, however, as he only said, "Yes, I'd thought to surprise you, but I'm too late, I see."

"Aye—we cut it a bit short, today, since donnybrooks were startin' to break out, left and right. Callie was there, and I invited her to dinner, but she shirked me off."

As they turned to resume the walk home, Acton offered in a mild tone, "I would only ask that you check-in with me first, Kathleen."

"I know—I'm sorry. She seemed a bit pulled-about, so I thought to break the ice, and start treatin' her like she's your sister, which she is."

There was a small pause. "Am I being scolded?"

"A bit."

He made no immediate response, as they walked along, and so she offered, "And—speakin' of new-found relatives—Callie tells me that Aunty Wickham has been tryin' to make inroads with her."

"Yes," he affirmed. "I didn't wish to alarm you."

Doyle blew out a breath. "Because that *is* a bit alarmin', Michael—that she'd go so far as to target Callie. My Aunty is a very thorough octopus, because I think she was doin' the same thing with Geary—tryin' to winkle-out some information about me, so as to help her out, in this charade. Munoz said that she pretended they'd met in Dublin, but Geary knew better."

He nodded. "There have been definite attempts to garner information, which is why I felt it important to warn Callie."

"Who doesn't necessarily appreciate it," Doyle observed.

"No; she thought me a bit heartless, I think, mainly because I could not tell her the true reason for the woman's attempts at friendliness."

She glanced up at him in sympathy. "No—and there's a prime dilemma, indeed; you've got to warn the girl, without warnin' her why. And you've got good reason not to tell her too much, because she's so resentful, just now, that she might just repeat anythin' you say right back to Wickham."

"Yes. It is a concern."

This seemed an opportune time to address something that had occurred to Doyle—something that would explain why Acton was more upset about this, than he was letting on.

Carefully, she offered, "In the normal course o' things, it shouldn't matter whether she's my aunt or not—major crimes have been committed, and that's that. But if the blacklegs on the Public Accounts Commission think my Aunty's little holy-show might help them, it might be an indication that they are well-aware you tend to sort things out to suit yourself, and can brush whatever you wish under the rug."

The thought was indeed alarming—the last needful thing was for these people to expose how Acton tended to do business—that tendency being not necessarily within the confines of the law.

But he seemed unconcerned about this potential aspect, and pointed out, "Don't forget that you are a very sympathetic figure, in your own right. Ms. Wickham would gain immediate leniency from the Crown Courts, if she were revealed as your only relative."

This only made sense, and she nodded—a bit ashamed that she'd been focused on her husband's looming disgrace, when this explanation was easily as plausible. "Right; I've my own immunity—lest we forget—and they're hopin' that I'll toss it over them, like Elisha-at-the-plow."

They walked a few more steps, and then she slowly shook her head. "I don't know, Michael—that doesn't seem quite right, either. If her claim as my Aunty is made public, then the news-people would suddenly be scrutinizin' that claim—which is as thin as tissue-paper—and she'd be exposed." She shook her head in confusion. "It all makes no sense—this whole pantomime seems passin' strange."

"Passin' strange," Edward repeated solemnly, because he was pretending to be part of the grown-up conversation.

Doyle laughed, and reached to clasp her son's arm, where it

was draped over his father's shoulder. "Well—whatever their plan is—it may soon be in ruins, if we can show that poor Yessenia's was a containment-murder. Did you have a chance to look into it?"

Acton raised his gaze, as their building loomed before them. "Her file shows that the suspect confessed, and so, there was no trial."

Doyle stared at him. "Faith, more octopuses, with their tentacles everywhere. And we'd never know the truth, save that her mother had the courage to go and speak to her killer."

"Indeed."

Reminded, Doyle asked, "Did you manage to get her mobile released? It may be cold comfort for her mum, but at least it's somethin'."

He tilted his head with regret. "Unfortunately, her mobile has been destroyed."

Doyle blinked. "I thought they were required to hang onto evidence for at least six months."

"You are correct."

She shook her head in wonder. "Mother a' *Mercy*, but these people are brassy. And so is my Aunty—small wonder, that you're frettin' six ways to Sunday."

But he immediately paused, to shift Edward to the other side so that he could lay a reassuring arm around her shoulders, and lower his head to hers. "No; instead I have matters well in hand, Kathleen—my promise on it. I am only deciding which route to take, so that there is as little fallout as possible."

This was a huge relief—since it was true—and it only made sense; this Public Accounts case—which now included the deaths of an MP, a whistleblower, and nine other innocent people—was obviously going to be very tricky to unwind, since it seemed clear that Acton felt he'd insufficient evidence to start arresting people, as yet.

She glanced up at him. "Do we tell Mary what we suspect about Howard's death?"

"I wouldn't, as yet," he advised. "She has enough to contend with."

"She does, indeed. Although d'you know who's come through with flyin' colors? Philippe Savoie, of all people. He's been drivin' her to Mass in the mornings, and helpin' out, as best he can. She says he calls the baby 'chow-choo', or some such thing."

"He would appear to have unexpected depths."

This, said with a discernable tinge of irony, which did not bode well for the necessary favor that Doyle was bound to ask. Nonetheless, she ventured, "Well, speakin' of which, Savoie was wonderin' if he could pay Reynolds to help Gemma and Emile with their homework, being as he's not very good at English grammar. It would be for an hour in the afternoons, whilst Mary's at home, nappin' with the baby."

Acton was silent, and so she made a face. "I know, I know— but Reynolds is willin', and I feel as though we've all got to pull the load, a bit."

"As long as they do not come to our flat. And you and Edward are to stay home," he decided. "You must rest, too."

"Aye, then; I'm sure that will be agreeable—it's probably easier for Emile to get over to Mary's place, anyways."

Hearing his hero's name, Edward lifted his head to inform his father, "Emile can jump, from the top of the monkey-bars!"

"But Edward knows that's too dangerous," Doyle reiterated, very firmly.

"Gemma knows, too," the little boy advised. "So, we only watched."

"Good one," Acton said, imitating Doyle.

The boy giggled. "Good one," he parroted, in his best Irish accent.

"No gangin' up on me," Doyle warned. "When Tommy's here, I'm goin' to be grossly outnumbered."

"I'll tell Tommy it's too dangerous," Edward offered. "He's too little."

With a twinkle, Doyle met her husband's eye, as the doorman opened the lobby door.

CHAPTER 17

That night, Doyle awoke around midnight—which was how things were, nowadays; it was almost impossible to find a comfortable position so as to sleep for more than a few hours at a time. With an effort, she shifted the pillow that cushioned her legs, and then was suddenly aware that her husband was not by her side.

After staring out the window at the night sky for a few moments, she slid out of bed, and then padded down the hallway to where a dim line of light could be seen, shining from beneath Acton's office door. With a quiet movement, she pushed the door open, and saw exactly what she'd expected to see; Acton leaning back in his chair, and gazing out the window, a glass of scotch cradled in his hands.

"May I come in?" she asked softly.

"You may," he said, glancing over at her. In the old days, he would try conceal the fact that he was drunk as a fiddler, but since she was never fooled, he no longer made the attempt.

She lowered herself into the chair across from his desk, and gazed out the window with him.

"I must apologize, Kathleen," he said, in the formal tones he used when he was bosky. "I thought I would have just one more glass, and then I lost track."

"Whist, you're well-entitled to have a tipple, when the house is finally quiet. Don't mind me."

They sat in silence for a few moments, and then she asked gently, "Can you tell me what's burdenin' you, Michael? If you're that angry at the doorman, for lettin' the door hit you today, I won't tell a soul."

He lowered his gaze to his glass. "If only it were that easy."

"Aye, the poor man would disappear, never to be seen again."

But he wouldn't be teased, and continued to contemplate his glass.

Oh-oh, she thought; I think it this far more serious than I thought, and shame on me, for not sorting it out sooner—whatever it is.

She ventured, "If you don't tell me, I'll presume you've a pretty girl on the side—one who still has a waist."

His chest rose and fell. "Believe it or not, there is a pretty girl."

"Is there?" asked Doyle in surprise, raising her brows. "Give me her ID, then; I'll get my gun, and be back within the hour."

He smiled slightly, but continued, "It's Callie."

Doyle blinked, as this was completely unexpected. "*Callie*? How so?"

He took a deep breath. "Callie has been—has been rather moody, lately."

Readily, Doyle agreed. "Aye—she's comin' to grips, Michael, and needs a bit o' time. It's not somethin' that you hear every day, and I think it's knocked her off her pins."

"It is—unfortunate, because when she behaves in this way, I find myself looking for my father in her, and I know that I shouldn't."

"Oh." The penny dropped; Acton's father had been a horror-show, cruel and despicable, and Acton was very vulnerable on the subject. Indeed, Doyle entertained the strong suspicion that Acton's more ruthless impulses were a direct result of his issues with his father—his outsized desire to bring the hammer down on any blacklegs, who were on the cusp of skating free.

Frowning, she thought about this, and then asked, "D'you look for my father in me?"

He smiled slightly. "No."

"Well, I don't look for yours in you, either. You're too obsessed with bloodlines, my friend, which is exactly what you get for bein' an aristocrat, and dwellin' on such things, day and night. It doesn't matter two pins, to God."

His chest rose and fell. "You have a very practical perspective."

"Well, it's true. And besides, you can't paint everyone with the same broad brush—it's miles more complicated than that; people are miles more complicated than that."

With a tilt of his head, he pointed out, "Their motives are not, though. We see the same motives, time and again."

She made a sound of reluctant agreement. "All right—I'll grant you that, I suppose. But Callie has no motive, surely?"

"She is resentful, I believe; resentful that she has lost her identity."

Making a wry mouth, Doyle observed, "Believe it or not, you're not the first person who's told me that a by-blow tends to be resentful. In this instance, though, I think it's more a combination of her bein' young, and a bit—a bit *overwhelmed* by it all. She'll find her feet; we only need to give her time."

She paused, much struck. "In a way, Callie's suffered the same blow that Mary has; her well-ordered life—all her plans—have suddenly been taken from her. Through no fault of her own, she's been plucked up, and placed somewhere other than where she was—even though to an outsider, it might seem that Callie's won the lottery."

"A good point, perhaps."

She smiled slightly. "Don't humor me, Michael—you know I hate it when you do. I guess that's not a very good comparison, with poor Mary having buried two good husbands, already."

"I don't know as they can be compared. Howard was far more worthy, than Blakney."

"Oh—I don't know, Michael; I think Blakney was a decent sort."

Before her husband could wonder how she would know such a thing, Doyle quickly moved on. "Your 'bloodlines' theory doesn't hold water, because even a blackleg can be a good father, and you need look no further than Philippe Savoie, as an excellent case-in-point."

He raised his head, to look at the window. "I am not certain that I can agree with that assessment."

She hid a smile, at his public-school tones, but insisted, "It's true, though; Savoie dotes on Emile—which is a shrine-worthy miracle, in its own right, when you think about where Emile sprang from. And Savoie's been kind to Mary and Gemma, mainly because his son loves them. I was just tellin' Williams that the man's turned a leaf, ever since he adopted Emile."

But her husband remained unconvinced. "You are optimistic, perhaps."

Gently teasing, she replied, "I don't know how else to be, my friend; recall that I am the ying to your yams."

He was silent, cradling his glass, and she was aware that he wanted to fill it up again, but was restrained by her presence. "I'll leave you to it, then," she offered, and made to rise. "But I promise that everythin' will look better in the mornin', Michael —it always does."

"One can hope."

At this answer, she paused at the doorway. "Oh-oh; shall I start stockpilin' ammo, and settin' up sandbags, at the windows?"

He shook his head slightly—as though to clear it—and quickly assured her, "No—I am sorry to alarm you, Kathleen. It is nothing that cannot be solved; I have only brought trouble upon myself, by being maladroit."

"Oh," she said. "If *that's* all."

He smiled slightly, as he gazed out the window. "It means that I have blundered."

"Have you? Well, welcome to my world, Michael."

She slipped out the door, and then made her way back toward the bedroom, thinking over what he'd said.

I'm not sure I'm buying it, she decided; he's very good at misdirection—shaving his words, so that they're mostly true, but not quite honest. And he's a past-master at sending me go off to fetch a random bone, so that I don't stumble-in on the real issue, which is what I think he's done this time.

So; what was the real issue? He said he was fretting about

Callie—and that part was true—but I'll bet my teeth there's more to it, than that. Callie is simply not that important, in Acton's world; it's not as though he suddenly loves her as a sister—and I don't think he's capable of such, in the first place.

So, I still haven't the faintest idea what's causing him to hole-up and drink himself silly, these past few nights. If I were guessing, I'd guess it has to do with my Aunty, because he doesn't like the fact my Aunty has shown up—doesn't like it a'tall—which is interesting, because, presumably, he can send her off with a flea in her ear, whenever he pleases. But for some reason, he's wary—warier than he should be, and it's causing him fits.

There had been occasions in the past, when Acton had lapsed into a black mood—terrible to behold—but she didn't have the impression that one of his black moods was hovering, this time. Instead—instead she'd the impression that he was frustrated, and he was not one who was used to being frustrated, being as he tended to do whatever he pleased, and the devil take the hindmost.

I think he's stymied about this whole Public Accounts case, and the fact he can't seem to roll-up Charbonneau, she decided. But that would be a first, because Acton's never stymied—or at least, never *this* stymied. Therefore, there must be something here that I don't understand about this massive tangle-patch, and how it all fits together. Williams knows something, but that gets me no further along, since Williams is not about to tell me whatever-it-is he knows. I will see him tomorrow, though, so mayhap I can make another attempt; I think it's important I find out, and the time that I have left to accomplish anything— whether important or not important—is rapidly running out.

I wonder, she thought, as she rather sleepily slid back into bed; I wonder if Williams knows how Reynolds met Charbonneau.

CHAPTER 18

$\mathcal{D}$oyle fell back to sleep, but she soon discovered that she was not slated to have a restful night, because she found herself having one of her dreams.

She had them, on occasion; strange, vivid dreams where she stood in darkness, outside on a rocky outcropping, with the wind blowing about her, even though she couldn't feel it against her skin. The dreams always featured another person— someone who was dead, but who was nevertheless tasked with giving her some sort of message, although the message was never very straightforward.

Overall, the dreams were a bit disturbing, but she'd learned, long ago, that she should pay attention, and try to puzzle-out why this particular person was attempting to convey a message to her. More than once, it had saved their lives.

This time, however, Doyle was truly confused, as she faced her ghostly visitor—a rather tough-looking man in his late thirties, who sported more than a few well-placed tattoos.

"You're to keep your nose out of it," the ghost warned in no uncertain terms. "He has things well in hand—women always make things more complicated than they need to be."

"Mr. Blakney," Doyle ventured. "You're mixed-up, I think; you're from a couple of ghosts back." She considered this. "Three, I think it is."

Bill Blakney was Mary's first husband—a pawn shop owner —and he'd first shown-up in Doyle's dreams to warn her to stay out of Reynold's plot to kill the Russian Colonel— although she hadn't realized that was his aim, until after the Colonel was already dead. As it turned out, Blakney heartily approved of the plot to kill the Russian, being as he loved little Gemma, too.

"You're to stay out of it," the ghost repeated, and crossed his muscled arms.

Hesitantly, Doyle ventured, "I think that's water under the bridge, Mr. Blakney—remember? Gemma's safe, and that's all been sorted-out."

He snorted. "Cripes, I don't know why everyone thinks you're so smart."

With a smile, Doyle replied, "You're definitely mixed-up, then; there's not a soul alive who thinks I'm smart."

"He does," the ghost countered, and bent his head so as to fix her with a knowing look.

There was a small pause. "Acton's frettin' to beat the band," she admitted. "But I haven't the first clue why. I truly don't think it's about Callie."

The ghost lifted a brow, and seemed amused. "Oh, yes, it is."

Doubtfully, she replied, "I truly don't think so, Mr. Blakney. She's just not that important to him—you don't know him like I do. No one's that important to him, save me. And Edward, too—but mainly because Edward's important to me."

"Exactly on the nail," her ghostly companion pronounced. "You've tied his hands, and he can't move one way or t'other. That's just fine—leave well-enough alone."

But Doyle frowned. "If he can't move, then how can you say he has things well-in-hand?"

"You're not following," the ghost replied. "But you don't need to; just back away."

With some bewilderment, she ventured, "How can I leave well-enough alone, if I don't know what the 'well-enough' is, in the first place? And I have to say, Mr. Blakney, that it doesn't seem very 'well' to me—Acton's been stewin' like a barleycorn, these past few days."

"His own fault," Blakney pronounced, without sympathy. "He was maladroit."

A bit crossly, she asked, "Why does everyone need to use a ten-pound word, when a two-pound one will do?"

"It means he made a tactical error, and now he's paying the price."

Slowly, she shook her head. "I haven't a clue, what you're talkin' about. Acton made an error with Callie? How so?"

"Maladroit," the ghost pronounced, savoring the word.

A bit exasperated, Doyle said, "Surely, he can set it all to rights? Acton's who he is, after all."

Nodding in pleased agreement, the ghost said, "Exactly. He has no choice, but to set it all to rights. That's why you're to stay out of it."

With no small confusion, Doyle ventured, "But you're not makin' any sense, Mr. Blakney; if it's always about me, why must I stay out of it? And if Acton's been mala—mala-something, why do you say he has things well in hand?"

Blakney chuckled. "Ha! Because he does—you can't catch him, he's the gingerbread man."

Nonplussed, Doyle stared at him. *"What?"*

But she was suddenly awake, her heart hammering, as she tried to catch her breath, alone in the bed.

CHAPTER 19

The next morning, Doyle sat for breakfast with Edward, whilst her husband prepared to leave for work. He looked none the worse for his night-drinking, which was a marvel; when Doyle worked alongside the fishmongers in Dublin, many a man could hardly stay upright, after a hard night out.

He leaned down to kiss her goodbye. "Text me at the slightest twinge," he teased.

"I will," she promised.

After hesitating a moment, he ran a hand over her head. "Promise me you'll not worry. I am trying to decide the best way forward, is all."

"Never doubted it," she replied stoutly.

Nevertheless, she duly noted that this seemed to contradict what the ghost had said—that he had things "well in hand." Was the ghost mistaken? Although this particular ghost kept contradicting himself, which wasn't very helpful—Acton was stymied, but Acton had things well in hand. Doyle was important, but Doyle had to stay out of it. It wasn't about Callie, but then again, it was.

There's something here I don't understand, she admitted to herself, as she watched Reynolds let her husband out the door. Not to mention that Blakney's definition of "well in hand" may not be the same as a law-abiding citizen's definition—there was always that. The man's pawn-shop had been ground-zero for some very questionable activities, and—lest we forget—he'd been all-in, on the Colonel's murder.

Which only brought up another, troubling point. Usually, the identity of the ghost was important, for some reason, but she couldn't think of any reason why Blakney was coming 'round, yet again, and telling the fair Doyle to mind her own business, yet again.

In fact, he'd been a notable exception, because usually, the ghosts who visited her dreams tended to badger her with a call-to-action. But instead, here was Blakney, badgering her to stand-down—although she couldn't very well stand-down, if she didn't even know what she was standing down from, in the first place. Which is exactly what happened last time, when Reynolds and Savoie had murdered the Colonel, before she'd caught wind of what was afoot.

So; why had Blakney returned? It made no sense—mayhap whoever was dispatching the ghosts had got them mixed-up, or something. Blakney, himself seemed plenty mixed-up, with his many contradictions—look no further than his parting shot; just as he was banging on about Acton's hands being tied, he suddenly changed his mind, and called him the gingerbread man—*can't catch me, I'm the gingerbread man.*

Which reminded her of yet another puzzler, in this mare'snest of them. "Reynolds," Doyle called out to the servant. "There's a word everyone keeps usin', and I'm not sure what it means. Mala-somethin'."

The servant paused in his kitchen duties to stand upright, thinking. "Malady, madam?"

"No. It's something that means a mistake, I think."

"Malaprop?" he suggested, and then added, almost kindly, "You mustn't take any criticisms to heart, madam."

She eyed him. "No—whatever that is, that's not it. And it's not about me, it's about Acton—he's the one who used it." She frowned, trying to remember. "Maladrome, or somethin' like that."

"Maladroit, madam?"

Doyle's brow cleared. "That's it; good one, Reynolds. What's it mean?"

"A French word, madam. It means the opposite of something done deftly."

"Ah," she said. "Thanks, Reynolds, that's clear-as-glass."

The servant hastily amended, "It means that something has been done in a clumsy fashion."

She stared at him. "Clumsy? Truly? Faith, that's hard to believe—Acton couldn't be clumsy, even if he practiced for days on end."

The butler was understandably at sea. "Perhaps more context is needed, madam."

But this was a rabbit-hole she knew she shouldn't go down, and so instead, she offered, "I just heard the word twice, yesterday. It's one of those surrender-dippity things."

"Indeed, madam," the butler said woodenly.

She smiled. "You should correct me, when I get it wrong, Reynolds; else I'll never learn."

"Serendipity, is the word I beleive you mean, madam."

"Oh—serendipity, then." Thoughtfully, she added, "It's like when you find out that there's an octopus, with its tentacles reachin' into the Public Accounts case, and then suddenly you think you see octopuses everywhere."

"I believe you mean 'octopi', madam."

Crossly, she advised, "I think 'octopuses' is a perfectly good word, Reynolds, and you don't have to correct me on *everything*. I'll thank you not to be the grammar-police."

"Very well, madam," the servant replied, in the manner of one who bears his long-suffering with great fortitude.

Immediately contrite, Doyle offered, "Sorry, Reynolds—pay no mind to my grouchy self. And I have to repent fastin', because Acton has given the go-ahead for the homework-plan, which makes you the grammar-police, in truth."

Reynolds brightened up. "Very good, madam."

Thinking to make amends, she added, "You did such a fine job, when we were takin' care of Emile, before. You'd have made a good schoolmaster, I'm thinkin'."

But this was a tactical mistake, as Reynolds only replied, "If you say, madam," in the tone of one who knows his own worth, as Lord Acton's personal butler.

Quickly moving forward, Doyle explained, "Acton asked if you could help them over at Mary's, though; he says he wants me to be able rest, when Edward's taking his nap."

"Just so, madam. You must reserve your strength."

Now there's some irony, she thought; I've a feeling that my strength is not slated to be reserved, anytime soon. Aloud, she said, "I'll get Mary's permission when I stop by this mornin', but I'm sure she'll have no objection—she'd probably love to have a lie-down, in the afternoons."

"I've made a lasagna to send over with you, madam."

"Thank you, Reynolds. I'm that sorry I snapped at you, and then called you a schoolmaster."

"Not at all, madam," the servant replied graciously. "I am often too exacting."

I'm exacting, too, in my own way, thought Doyle, as she prepared to take her leave, and kissed Edward goodbye. But only because things niggle at me and I know—from massive experience—that there's always a good reason they do.

Therefore, as she walked toward the lift, she rang up Yessenia's mother. "Hello ma'am; I was wondering if we could meet-up? I'd like to give you an update."

"Of course, Officer Doyle—I'm home all morning."

Doyle jotted down the address, and thoughtfully leaned back against wall in the lift, as it made its hushed way down to the lobby. Yesterday, she'd noted a funny little nuance in Acton's voice, when he'd told her that the dead girl's phone had been destroyed; better see if the mother had any idea about what that phone might have contained.

The doors slid open, and—with stoic determination—she straightened up, scolding herself for entertaining the idea that she'd almost welcome labor, just so as to have an excuse to go back to bed, and pull the covers over her head.

CHAPTER 20

"You'll be happy to hear that our Callie is goin' to return to the land of the livin'," Doyle disclosed to Adrian, as he drove her over to Mary's flat. "She told me she'll be at Mary's this mornin', so as to give Lizzie a break. Hold a good thought that the poor girl has righted herself, and is on the mend."

Adrian replied, "I hope so, ma'am. She's been very unhappy, and I think it's because—" he paused, and then said, "Well, maybe I shouldn't say."

With some interest, Doyle leaned forward as far as her girth would allow. "Of course, you should, Adrian. I won't tell her you said, and if we can help to straighten her out, the more power to us."

Adrian disclosed, "I think she fell rather hard for that French fellow—the one she sees at the playground."

There was a moment of surprised silence. "Savoie?" Doyle had to smile in amusement, as she slowly sank back in the seat.

"Faith, I suppose that's not a wonder—even Callie's mother was crushin' on Savoie. What is it with women, and dangerous men?"

Adrian smiled a bit ruefully. "Exactly."

"Well, not to worry, it's not goin' anywhere—even though I imagine Savoie would get an enormous kick out of puttin' Acton into such a situation—can you imagine?"

Oh, she thought suddenly, oh—wait; there's something here, something rather dark—

"She'll get over it," Adrian agreed.

"She doesn't have much choice," Doyle replied absently. "And she'll be needin' a sympathetic man, to pick up the pieces."

Whilst Adrian flashed his smile at this ham-handed attempt at matchmaking, Doyle closed her eyes for a moment, trying to catch at the elusive thought. What was it? Surely, Savoie wouldn't take advantage of Callie? No—it would never happen, mainly because Savoie wouldn't rock the boat, for such a petty reason. He'd a good thing going, with his partner-in-crime being a renowned Chief Inspector—one who was willing to throw his own mantle of immunity over the Frenchman's misdeeds, with the murder of that Russian Colonel coming straight to mind. And besides, Savoie wasn't the type to dally with a younger lass like Callie—although truth to tell, most men would need very little encouragement. Not Savoie, though—although she wasn't sure why she knew this, with such certainty.

I should probably speak with Callie about it, Doyle decided with some resignation—although I'm not the best person to give love-advice, and she'll not thank me for putting my foot in. But there's something here—another wretched niggle—and

I suppose I should take up my own mantle, like a good sister would.

Adrian was enlisted to carry up the lasagna to Mary's flat, and—upon sighting Callie—he started chatting with her, which seemed a hopeful turn of events, and so Doyle ushered Mary into the kitchen, so as to give the other two a bit of privacy.

"Let's make tea and coffee," she suggested, and then was surprised to behold a fancy new coffee-making device on the counter. "Will you look at this? I'm afraid it will take a finger off, if I'm not careful."

Mary explained, "Philippe brought it in—he likes espresso, and he says he needs it to stay awake, when he helps with the homework." She smiled. "As for me, I'll take plain tea, any day."

"Well, I don't dare try it, for fear I'll drink a gallon, and give this poor baby a fine case of the willies."

Mary chuckled. "How are you feeling, Lady Acton? It doesn't seem so long ago that I was in your condition."

"I'm as well as can be," Doyle offered, and noted that the widow seemed a little brighter, than she'd been the last visit. Thank all available saints, she thought, that Father John was not afraid to wade into grief, and help to pull you through it. No one knows this better than me, and my hat's off to him.

"I will make your coffee, Lady Acton; you should sit down."

"No—I'm happy to stand, for a bit," Doyle lied, being as she could hear Callie and Adrian, still talking in the next room. "But—speakin' of the homework—we've hatched a plan, and we'll need your permission."

Mary lifted her brows, as she took the kettle from the stove. "Oh? What sort of plan?"

"Savoie doesn't mind helpin' Emile and Gemma do their homework, but he's not at the top, with respect to the English-grammar part, and so Reynolds has volunteered to help with the homework, instead. He'll come over, whilst me and Edward are nappin' at home."

"Oh—" Mary protested in dismay.

"Not a word," Doyle admonished. "It will give you some quiet time for a lie-down with Hannah, and you know Reynolds will be in his glory."

There was a pause. "All right, then—but it's only temporary."

"For heaven's sake, Mary—enough; we're all happy to help. And this way, poor non-English Savoie can go home, and drink his espresso in peace."

Mary glanced at the clock. "He'll be by later—today's the day he helps me order the groceries for the week."

Doyle blinked. "Never say Savoie is fetchin' groceries?"

Mary chuckled. "No—that's a hard one to imagine, isn't it? He has a service, though, and he says it makes everything much more convenient, which it does." She paused, and then added, "I think it's expensive, though. He offered to pay for Gemma's school, too, but I told him you'd already taken care of it." She paused, and her lip trembled a bit. "Everyone has been so generous, so very kind—"

Hastily, Doyle set down her coffee cup, and gently put her arms around the other woman, as she cried into the kitchen towel for a few moments.

"Whist," said Doyle softly. "There's no point to havin' friends, unless you put them to good use."

Straightening up, Mary wiped her eyes. "Yes. Thank you, Lady Acton—I am so lucky, to have you all. My brother in

Leeds offered to take us in—he's got a houseful, himself, but I told him that we're set, for the time being, and I'd hate to pull Gemma out of her school."

"Aye, the lass seems to be handlin' everythin' as well as can be."

"Yes—she's doing just fine, which is one of the reasons I was hoping to keep up our usual routine." She paused. "Nigel —Nigel was a good father, but he had plenty of late nights— especially lately—and so, he wasn't able to spend as much time with Gemma as he wished. She asks after him, and we say our prayers together, but it hasn't seemed to affect her, very much."

Mary bit her lip, before it trembled again, and Doyle offered, "Children are so resilient, Mary. It's a blessin', is what it is. And their grief would be ours, so it's one less burden."

"Yes," Mary agreed, and quickly wiped her eyes. "Is there anything I should have ready for Reynolds?"

"He'll see to everythin', Mary—you know how he is." Doyle checked the time. "I've got to interview some witnesses this mornin', but I'll be sure to tell Reynolds and Savoie that the homework plan is a go."

"I will see Philippe later today," Mary reminded her.

"Right, then; although they'll need to coordinate, to get Emile over here." Doyle smiled in farewell. "Give Hannah a kiss, when she wakes—cheers, Mary; although that may not be the best thing to say."

Mary smiled. "The Lord loves a cheerful giver."

Aye, Doyle thought, as she went back into the sitting room; and you know who are the cheerful givers, here? Savoie and Reynolds, that's who, whereas I am more of a grouchy giver— faith, I need to step-up my game. Although I've never conspired to murder anyone, like the two of them have, so I suppose there's a point to me.

"Come along, Adrian," Doyle announced. "I've got to go interview some witnesses, and since Williams is meetin' me, I can't be late—don't want him to give me the sack."

"Where to?" asked Adrian cheerfully, because he wanted to demonstrate to Callie what an amiable fellow he was.

"Griffin Transport Company—I think it's over in Old Oak."

"I'll look it up, ma'am."

"Goodbye Callie—don't forget to come over for dinner, soon."

"I'll look forward to it," the girl replied, and this was not exactly true.

CHAPTER 21

*O*nce she'd arrived at the transport company's headquarters, Doyle dismissed Adrian—being as she'd hitch a ride home with Williams—and then waited on the pavement out front, since she was early, for a change, and Williams had texted that he was on his way.

As she waited, she closed her eyes briefly, and breathed in the morning air—it looked to be a fine, sunny day. And—just as she'd told Acton—things did look much more encouraging, in the light of day. Mary was doing better every time Doyle saw her, and Callie had returned to her post—thank God fastin', because Edward was a handful, and best handled in shifts. Especially nowadays, when he thought it was hilarious to run away, just like the gingerbread man. Of course, the gingerbread man eventually came to a bad end, but that didn't seem to dampen Edward's enthusiasm one tiny whit.

So; poor Reynolds would hand over Edward duties to Callie —although now he'd have another chore, what with the homework sessions. He'd not mind it, though; he seemed to enjoy it, last time he'd been recruited, and, of course, he'd love to spend some quality-time with little Gemma. Reynolds was very fond of Mary's stepdaughter, which was why he'd done something so completely unexpected, and had asked Savoie if he'd please kill the Colonel, so as to solve all problems.

It just goes to show that you never know, she thought; love is so completely unpredictable, and I'm the poster-child for it. Or more properly, Acton is the poster-child for it, since never in a million years would the man have believed he'd wind up moving heaven and earth to please a rookie detective, fresh off the boat from Ireland.

She paused, because her scalp had started prickling, and whilst she pondered why it would—Acton lived to please her, and that wasn't much of a news-flash—she was hailed by a familiar voice.

"Kathleen; I thought that was you. I hope you don't mind."

Casually, she turned to greet her false Aunty Wickham, and mentally castigated herself, because Acton was going to blister Adrian up one side and down the other for leaving her alone, before Williams showed up. Although it was possible that it was Adrian, who'd given the woman her location, in which case Doyle would be happy to blister him, herself; it seemed very unlikely that this was a chance encounter, here in the wilds of the Old Oak industrial area.

"Hallo," said Doyle easily. "I'm afraid I can't chat, as I'm on-duty."

"Of course—forgive me, but I thought I recognized the driver, and I couldn't resist seeing if it was you."

This was false, which was expected, but Doyle was more interested in the fact that—despite this unlooked-for annoyance

—she felt rather sorry for the woman who was standing before her. I wonder why they're putting her up to this, she thought, and I wonder whether I can bend down far enough to pull my gun from its ankle-holster, if need be.

Ruefully, the woman grimaced. "I hadn't heard from you, and I am so very sorry if I've upset you. Believe me, that was not my intent."

Remembering Acton's instruction, Doyle pretended to think this over. "I'll hear what you have to say, I suppose, but not just now, of course. Give me a few days, and I'll get in touch."

But the other pleaded, "Is there any chance we can meet after work, today? I've so much to tell you—about your Uncle John, and all your cousins."

Whilst Doyle tried to think of the proper response to this mention of completely fictitious people, she was fortunately spared, since Williams strode-up, very quickly.

"Ma'am," he said, with a nod to the false aunt. "Sergeant; if this is a witness, we'll need a more secure venue."

"No, sir," said Doyle, with a show of being discomfited. "She's just an acquaintance, who happened by."

With a chiding glance at Doyle, Williams said to the woman, "I'm sorry ma'am, but you'll have to clear out; this is police business."

"I beg your pardon," Wickham said apologetically, even as she emanated waves of chagrin. To Doyle, she offered in a humble tone, "I will be in touch, Kathleen."

"Let's go in," said Williams briskly, and as they turned to mount the steps, he said under his breath, "Are you all right?"

"I am," Doyle replied.

"That's the one, isn't it?"

"It is."

"Do you need to phone Acton?"

"I'd be very much surprised if he wasn't already tracin' her, but let me phone, just in case this was unexpected."

With Williams keeping a sharp eye out, Doyle paused outside the company's front door to ring-up Acton on their private line, and he answered immediately.

"Kathleen."

"Aunty just approached me, out of the blue."

There was a slight pause. "You're at Old Oak Common?"

"I am."

"Williams is there?"

"Aye. And I must say, Michael, your skills are fadin', if you weren't keepin' track of the wretched woman."

Apologetically, he explained, "I put a transponder on her vehicle, but she may have switched cars. I must go; I will see if I can trace her."

"Cheers."

"Christ," said Williams, who'd been listening to her side of the conversation. "She could have had a weapon, Kath."

Doyle sheathed her phone. "Don't let Father John hear you blaspheme, my friend. And—strange as it may seem—I felt a bit sorry for her. She's gettin' nowhere, and she must have known I wouldn't much like bein' buttonholed, like this."

A bit grimly, he replied, "She'll about to get buttonholed into prison."

But Doyle pointed out, "There's nothing to charge her with, Thomas. She hasn't tried to trick me into givin' her money, or anythin'. Her counsel would just argue that she's delusional, and besides, it would never even get that far, because Acton is not about to go public about this."

Much struck, she added, "You know, I think whoever's

behind this odd little catfishin' operation—Charbonneau, presumably—knows exactly that. She knows that Acton stays under the radar, at all costs, and so she's usin' that against him."

"Maybe," he agreed. "He likes to stay private."

"He's the king of private—the Holy Roman Emperor," she affirmed.

Williams took a quick survey of the area, and then said, "Let's go in; I don't like to think that your aunt is still watching you."

But Doyle remembered what she'd wanted to ask him, and stayed him, with a hand on his arm. "D'you know how Reynolds knows Charbonneau?"

He stared at her in abject surprise. "*Reynolds* knows *Charbonneau?*"

She smiled at his reaction. "Obviously, the answer is 'no'."

Incredulous, he ventured, "Do you think Reynolds is compromised?"

"No," she said with complete certainty. "But he's acquainted with Charbonneau, somehow, and doesn't want to tell me how that came about."

Williams frowned, thinking about it. "Acton may have used him as a lure."

Doyle nodded. "That's what I was thinkin'—and that's why I thought mayhap you'd know the answer."

"I don't, but it almost doesn't matter, Kath; Acton needs to go hard after Charbonneau—this thing with the aunt seems dangerous."

But Doyle spread her hands. "He can't touch Charbonneau, just the same as he can't touch my Aunty. There's no such crime, as a conspiracy to present false relatives—not unless somethin's bein' stolen. And Charbonneau is a CI, lest we forget."

Williams countered, "I wasn't necessarily speaking of having her arrested; Acton has other ways of sending a message."

This remark gave her pause, because this was undeniably true—and Williams knew of which he spoke, because many a time, he was Acton's henchman, in the message-sending.

Slowly, she replied, "Aye—that's the truth. But I think he's stymied about what to do with her, for some reason."

She could suddenly sense Williams' wariness, and she was reminded that he knew more about this than he was letting on. Eying him narrowly, she asked, "If I'm in danger, Thomas Williams, I would think that's good enough reason for you to unsnabble, and tell me what you know about all this."

"I can't," he replied, nettled. "And you're better off not knowing—believe me."

"Allow me to be the judge of that, my friend."

But Williams turned the subject—in true Williams fashion—and countered, "Why were you left alone, just now?"

She made a face. "Don't worry, I was wonderin' the same thing. But to be fair, I did dismiss Adrian, even though he shouldn't have left me until you came." She paused, and then admitted, "On the other hand, Adrian may have told my Aunty that I was goin' to be here, since he knew where we were goin'."

He met her eyes in alarm. "Do you think your driver's in on it? Acton should be told."

She sighed, debating this. "I'd have a hard time, believin' Adrian would do somethin' malicious, Thomas, but it's possible he was talked into it—he's a bit naïve, I think. Let me speak to him, before bringin' in Acton—I can sort-out the truth, after all."

He tilted his head in a cautionary movement. "Just don't take any chances, Kath."

Annoyed, she retorted, "Well, thanks for nothin', Thomas Williams; I've been left in the dark, so I can't know whether I'm takin' a chance or not, and I don't much appreciate havin' to fly blind."

He let out a breath, and ran his hands through his hair. "Don't be angry, Kath. It's not just about you and me, any more."

With some dismay, she remembered that he'd made a previous remark about keeping his family safe, and— immediately contrite—she offered, "I'm that sorry, Thomas; and you're right—you have to think of Lizzie and that little boyo of yours, who are much higher in the peckin'-order than the likes of me."

"My gooseberry-baby," he joked, trying to return to a more comfortable footing. "Lizzie and I are leaning toward not telling him—not telling Connor, about his mother."

She made a wry mouth. "I'll admit I've no idea what you should do, what with Callie's situation so close to mind. Although she's a bit of a cautionary tale, my friend; she learned the truth, all in a rush, and it's definitely not goin' smoothly."

He nodded, no doubt having heard chapter-and-verse from Lizzie. "You'd think it wouldn't be such a terrible thing, to find out you are Acton's sister."

But she pointed out fairly, "I don't know, Thomas; we get a big sense of who we are, from our family. Imagine findin' out that you're somethin' other than what you've always believed.

It would shake you to the core, and you could easily resent the people who knew all along, but didn't see fit to tell you."

"That's the downside," he admitted.

She reached to squeeze his arm in sympathy. "The downside doesn't hold a candle to the upside, though."

"Exactly," he agreed, with an answering smile. "Shall we go in?"

CHAPTER 22

They approached the front desk, where it was clear that the receptionist was expecting them. "Oh, yes, Officers; of course, we'd like to help in any way we can—such an awful thing to have happened."

"You were surprised to hear it?" asked Williams.

The young woman nodded. "Everyone was. And it's so very sad, because we all wondered why we didn't sense that he was so unhappy—we could have got him into counseling. The company would have paid for it, after all."

"Did you know Enrique well?"

She considered. "Not as well as the chaps in the back—the drivers, and the other guards. The office staff doesn't interact with the warehouse personnel, as much."

"I'd like to speak to some of the men he worked with—it should only take a few minutes."

"Of course," she said as she pressed a button that allowed the security door to open. "This is a good time, because the

130

trucks are here, mostly. We avoid morning drives, because we don't like to get stuck in traffic."

She led them into the cavernous, echoing warehouse, where a dozen transport trucks were lined up, behind the closed warehouse doors. A few men sat at a break-table off to the side, and they regarded the two detectives with open curiosity, when the receptionist gestured them their way.

As they approached, Doyle made the usual assessments a detective makes when sizing-up witnesses. No one has anything to hide, she decided. They're relaxed, and curious— not a'tall alarmed, by the brace of detectives who've shown up on their doorstep.

Williams began, "We'd like to ask a few questions about Enrique, if you don't mind."

"Ask away," said one man. "Although I'm not sure there's much we can say; we were all blown away by the news."

"Has he ever shown signs of violence? Did he have a temper?"

"No," the spokesman said flatly. "I mean, he could take care of himself, if we got into a pub-scuffle, or something, but he wasn't aggro." He paused, and then added, "Besides, they'd never let him work here, if he didn't keep his nose clean."

Williams nodded. "Did he ever grouse about his girlfriend?"

The others stared at him for a moment, and one man was seen to duck his head, and smile behind his hand.

The spokesman offered, "You lot are barking up the wrong tree, officer. He wasn't much interested in women, if you know what I mean."

There was a small, profound silence, and then Williams said, "I want to make certain we are talking about the same person." On his phone, he pulled up a snap of the decedent, and showed it to them.

"Yeah, that's him." The others all nodded.

Williams closed the photo, and offered in a neutral tone, "It appears that he was living with a woman, and there was a domestic dispute that resulted in a murder-suicide."

The others all stared in surprise, and the spokesman offered, "Really? I always had the sense he lived alone—he never mentioned a roommate to me. He had friends, of course."

Williams poised his pen. "Can you give me any information about his friends?"

The spokesman tilted his head in apology. "I don't know much—he kept that part of his life to himself. Although we did kid him about the pretty girl—we said it was such a waste."

The others nodded and chuckled, as Williams knit his brow. "Tell me about this—do you know the pretty girl's name?"

"No. Poor thing; she was so smitten, that she came in, and wanted to talk to him—a month or so ago, it was."

"Can you describe her?"

The spokesman made the universally-recognized sound of male appreciation. "Pretty, long hair. She looked Hispanic. Dark hair, slim."

Since "slim" wouldn't describe the female victim at the flat, Williams was seen to pause. "How old, do you think?"

The spokesman looked at the other men, and together, they guessed, "Twenty-one? Twenty-two?"

Oh, thought Doyle suddenly. Oh—

Williams asked, "Would the receptionist know her name?"

But Doyle found that she already knew the pretty girl's

name, and whispered it, over the roaring sound in her ears. "Yessenia. Yessenia Moreno."

Williams glanced at her in surprise, as the witness said, "Oh, was that it? He wouldn't tell us, no matter how much we razzed him. She wanted to talk to him here, but it's a secure area, so he went out for a walk with her." He smiled in amusement. "She never came back."

"Did you hear anythin' that she said to him?" asked Doyle.

He shrugged. "It wouldn't matter; I don't speak Spanish."

"She'll be on surveillance tape, right?" asked Williams, as he took a note.

"Of course, but she wasn't anyone suspicious—just a pretty, young woman."

"If you would give us a minute, please."

As could be expected, Williams was itching for a private conversation with his support officer about what she knew about these events, but as Doyle pretended to take a note, she whispered under her breath, "Code Four." The police code was the one used when an assignment was wrapping up, and the officers were vacating the premises.

To his credit, Williams didn't skip a beat, but walked back to the men, and said, "Thanks so much. We will be in touch, if we need any further information. And if you hear anything, call me; here's my card."

On the way back to the car, Doyle immediately pulled her mobile to phone Acton, but then remembered he'd his hands full with her stupid Aunty, and so instead, she texted: "When you're free."

"Let's hear it," said Williams, as soon as the car door was closed.

"Enrique wasn't a murderer, Thomas. Instead, he was

another containment-murder—I'm almost certain of it. I think Yessenia was the pretty Spanish girl who came to speak to him —she was the whistleblower, in the tainted-medication case, remember? And now we have someone she contacted, who winds up in a similar situation; the official homicide report is not a'tall what actually happened, and this victim—who was interactin' with Yessenia—is now conveniently dead, with the case-file about to firmly close."

Williams blew out a breath. "Which means we can presume Enrique must have known something about the tainted-medication case, too."

"Aye. I wonder if the villains were usin' this transport company—mayhap to deliver the pharmaceuticals? Mayhap Enrique noticed somethin' amiss?"

"Possibly," he agreed.

Doyle offered, "And I'll bet my teeth that it was Charbonneau, who called-in the supposed domestic dispute, Thomas. She was settin' the stage for a graveyard-love case, so that we wouldn't pay very much attention to it."

He added, "The same way a drug-fight homicide doesn't attract much attention."

"Oh," she breathed, "Oh—you're right."

Indeed, this was an unfortunate truth, in homicide work; if the victim was a criminal involved in criminal acts, there wouldn't be a lot of hand-wringing amongst the law-enforcement types, and the case would be given short shrift. The same could be said for a graveyard-love case, where the perpetrator's motive would be obvious. Therefore, these two containment-murders had been disguised to look like run-of-the-mill cases, so as to avoid a more thorough evaluation.

Struck with an idea, she offered, "On the other hand, it

might give us a path to pin somethin' on Charbonneau—obstruction of justice, mayhap. We can listen to the tip-line tape, and try to prove it was Charbonneau, by voice-recognition."

But he met her eyes, the expression in his own skeptical. "She's a CI, Kath. She would only say that she was calling-in a tip on behalf of someone who wanted to stay anonymous. That's what a CI does."

"Oh. I suppose you're right." Deflated, she blew out a breath. "Frustratin', is what this is—she's a slippery little eel."

Williams started the car. "All right; let's go back, and talk to Acton about how to handle this."

In a casual tone, she asked, "Would you mind, if I go for a quick check-in with Yessenia's mum? I told her I'd be by, and give her an update. It shouldn't take a mo', Thomas, and you can stay in the car, if you'd rather not go in."

He seemed hesitant, and so she added, "Acton's still busy tryin' to trace my Aunty, else he would have called me back. I promise that it won't take long, and when I do hear from him, I'll be out like a shot."

"You can't tell Yessenia's mother about our working-theory, Kath," he warned. "Or else, she might be the next containment-murder."

"Don't worry—I'll be careful. But I told her I'd check-in, and so I'd like to."

She gave the address, and he entered it into his navigation system. They drove in silence for a few moments, and then he slowly shook his head. "Wow."

"Exactly my thought," she agreed.

CHAPTER 23

*D*oyle sat with Yessenia's mother at the woman's kitchen table, and explained, "I'm workin' on untanglin' this strange mix-up, ma'am, but—since it may involve police corruption—I've got to keep it very quiet. You mustn't say anythin' to anyone—it's very, very important."

"Yes," the woman agreed, her eyes wide. "I understand, Officer Doyle."

"And I'm workin' on gettin' Yessenia's phone back, but I can't make it too obvious that I'm suspicious about anythin'. I have to make it look like a routine request, and so it may take a bit more time."

"Thank you," the woman said. "I would like to have her phone." She paused, and then absently wiped the tears from her eyes, as though she wasn't even aware that she did so, anymore. "She took a lot of snaps—like they do, the young ones. Always so happy."

Doyle's phone pinged, but Doyle ignored it for a moment.

"Did Yessenia happen to show you anythin'—well, anythin' *unusual* that was on her phone? D'you know if she took any snaps of documents, or anythin' like that?"

The girl's mother looked at her a bit blankly. "No, Officer Doyle. She would show me her snaps, sometimes—show me the people she would talk about."

Thinking of Enrique, Doyle pressed, "Did she talk about any new friends, that she'd met recently?"

The woman smiled slightly. "She is friends with your friend, Officer Doyle. She showed me a photo she took with her, because she knew I would enjoy it."

Doyle blinked. "*My* friend?"

"Yes—the woman you rescued; I can't remember her name. My Yessenia met her at an outreach event—they were trying to recruit minority women."

"Munoz," said Doyle slowly. "Officer Munoz."

Whilst the woman described the encounter, Doyle half-listened, as she tried to tamp down her alarm. Was it a coincidence, that Munoz had recently met the victim, and then Munoz's husband had botched her case? But surely, *surely* Munoz didn't know anything about the containment murders —she'd not stand idly by, if she knew such a thing was happening.

Unless—unless she was covering for Geary, mayhap— Munoz had a family to protect now, too. *Could* Geary be involved?

Frowning, Doyle stared at the opposite wall for a moment, and tried to decide if such a thing was possible. She tended to believe the best in everyone, after all, and sometimes it made her miss the warning signs. As an excellent case-in-point, she'd no idea until after she'd married her husband that he was rather ruthless, when it came to sorting things out, so as to suit his own notions of justice.

Her scalp started prickling, and she closed her eyes, trying to decide why it would. Surely, Geary wasn't ruthless, too? It didn't seem at all in keeping, with the man. Then who was? Charbonneau seemed ruthless—nearly as ruthless as Acton, when you thought about the murder of Howard, in the faint hope of saving her own skin. And these awful containment-murders were as ruthless as it got—no one would have ever known, save for Yessenia's mother, here, who'd been willing to talk to her daughter's killer, so as to try to find a light in the darkness.

Her companion broke off in some alarm, and reached to place a hand on Doyle's arm. "Officer Doyle, are you feeling all right? Do you need to lie down?"

Smiling, Doyle brought her attention back to the woman. "No—no, I'm feelin' fine; I was just thinkin' about—about everythin'." Her mobile pinged again, and she decided she'd best reply to Acton's text. "Excuse me," she said, and then texted, "OK call U in a mo."

Rising heavily to her feet, Doyle bade the witness goodbye, and reiterated, "Remember that you mustn't tell anyone about the murder mix-up—don't forget."

"I won't," the woman promised, as they walked to the door. "Thank you, Officer Doyle."

I hope I'm worthy of being thanked, when all's said and done, thought Doyle, as she walked out; the shades-of-grey are rolling in, thick and fast, so as to cloud everything up. Ironic, it is, that I was just sitting atop my high horse, and lecturing Williams about such things.

As she approached the waiting unmarked, she rang-up

Acton. "Michael; just let me get in the car, before I fill you in. Williams and I are crime-solvin' to beat the band."

"Are you? I wish I were."

"Well, that's disappointin'. You can't find Aunty?"

"I will," he assured her, and it was true.

I wish I had one-tenth of his confidence, she thought, as she wriggled into the passenger seat. Although I suppose most of it stems from that aforementioned ruthlessness; he's not one to give up, or give in.

After she shut the door behind her, she revealed to her husband, "We went to speak to the graveyard-love suspect's employer, and it turns out that Yessenia had made contact with him at work, a few weeks ago."

There was a pause. "That is interesting, indeed. Is there surveillance tape?"

"There should be—it's a transport company. She came over, and pestered him until they went on a walk. And there's more; the other workers said he hadn't a girlfriend, because he didn't fish from that side of the river."

"Ah," her husband said.

Into the silence, Doyle added, "So, the graveyard-love scene was staged, just like Yessenia's was—another containment-murder, it looks like."

"Very good work; I must go—would you put Williams on?"

Doyle dutifully handed her phone to Williams, who listened to whatever Acton wanted to tell him without comment—probably that he was to stick to the man's wife like a burr, so that there was no chance Aunty could make any further attempts.

Whilst her companion was thus occupied, Doyle gazed at the street scene through the windscreen, and contemplated the unsettling fact that Acton couldn't seem to trace her false Aunty. Although—come to think of it—that wasn't exactly what he'd said, of course, because he was the grand-master at shading his words, so as to throw her off.

Faith; I'll bet my teeth he knows exactly where the wretched Ms. Wickham is, she decided. He's got access to all the Yard's bells-and-whistles, after all, and it only stands to reason—he's always got his finger on the pulse of all things underworld. But if he's indeed monitoring the woman, to see where she goes, then why wouldn't he just *tell* me? It's not like it isn't routine CID procedure, to see who the unsuspecting-suspect associates with, so as to toss a wider net. Why won't he just say?

With a mental sigh, she turned her mind to her other, more pressing problem; she hadn't mentioned Yessenia's phone to Acton, because she held the rather unsettling suspicion that he'd destroyed the phone, himself. He didn't want the fair Doyle to find out what was in it—presumably, the victim's snap with Munoz. Which might mean that Acton knew that Geary had thrown-in with the blacklegs—after all, they already knew that Geary had consorted with her Aunty, even though he claimed that he'd rebuffed her. It would also explain why Acton was being so mysterious about everything; his wife had only a handful of close friends, and he'd move heaven and earth, to try to save them from ruin—not necessarily for their own sakes, but for hers.

But try as she might, Doyle couldn't quite talk herself into this working-theory. "It just doesn't make any sense," she mused aloud.

"What doesn't?" Williams asked, as he handed her mobile back.

Doyle closed her eyes briefly, trying to decide how much

Williams should be told—after all, he and Munoz and Geary were all friends, too.

Coming to a decision, she replied, "I think we should talk to Munoz, Thomas. Can you ring her up, and put together a case-management conference?"

Williams, who was no fool, gave her a sharp glance. "What's up?"

Slowly, she asked, "Is it *possible* that Geary is involved in these containment-murders?"

Quietly, he replied, "I would be very surprised."

His reaction told her that he'd already pursued this line of reasoning on his own, which just went to show you that Williams was also very good at playing his cards close to his vest. She should watch and learn, but on the other hand, she'd an impressive record of solving cases using her own tromping-about style, and allowing the cards to fall where they may.

"I'd be surprised, too," she agreed. "On the other hand, it's hard to believe Geary would botch a case so badly, even if he was relying on evidence from Charbonneau-the-crooked-CI. The CIs may give us leads, but everyone knows not to rely on them for outright evidence."

"I'll agree," he said.

"So, I'd like to speak with Munoz, if you wouldn't mind."

"You may put her in a bind," he warned.

But Doyle wasn't having it. "Fah, Thomas—listen to yourself, will you? If Geary is aidin' and abettin' containment-murders, he's got to be stopped; we can't stand aside just because he's our friend—and Munoz is, too. Nobody has immunity to commit murder."

But in an ironic tone, he only replied, "I could name a few," and then started the car.

CHAPTER 24

*O*nce back at Williams' office, Munoz was duly summoned, and as Doyle lowered herself into one of the chairs, she tried to decide how this particular interrogation should be handled. "Should I speak to her alone, d'you think?"

"Let's bring her up to date, first," Williams replied, as he opened-up his laptop.

"How much do we say, though?" Doyle ventured.

He considered this, and decided, "I vote we treat this like any other case. Acton can handle the Geary-angle, but as for us, we've got a case to close."

"Right," she agreed, a bit reluctantly. "Although we're a lot further away from closin' it than we thought, if the new workin' theory is that Charbonneau staged it." Thinking about this, she grimaced. "And I suppose that also means that the poor female victim was mindin' her own business in her kitchen, but wound up dead, because she was in the wrong place, at the wrong time."

"She did have a record," Williams noted. "Petty stuff. Not that she deserved to die, of course."

Doyle, who hadn't yet signed-off on the preliminary report —she should do it today, mental note—frowned at this. "What sort of petty stuff?"

He gave her a look. "Previous job was at a coin shop, in Bristol."

"Ah," said Doyle. "Say no more." Coin shops, like pawn shops, were notorious as fronts for money-laundering, and the fact that it was located in Bristol only served as petty-crime confirmation of this unfortunate fact.

"Here's Munoz," he said, and buzzed her in.

After the other detective drew up a chair, Williams began, "We've an update, on the graveyard-love case. We got a lead, from the male victim's co-workers."

Munoz took out her tablet, and prepared to take notes. "Good. You had better luck than I did—I learned nothing, when I spoke to the female victim's co-workers at the bakery. They're a dodgy bunch, I might add."

"She did have a record," Doyle piped up, so that she didn't look wholly ignorant.

Munoz nodded. "Yes, I think a lot of them do. That bakery is one of the businesses that cooperates with the Parole Board, in giving parolees a job. No one wanted to talk to me—I felt as though I was canvassing at the projects."

Williams continued, "Our update is that it turns out that there's a connection between the male victim, and a closed homicide case."

"Oh?" said Munoz, raising her brows. "He'd already killed someone?"

"No—he was recently seen speaking with Yessenia Moreno,

143

who then became a homicide victim herself, in an apparently unrelated case."

The words were said in a neutral tone, but Munoz reacted immediately, as she slowly lowered her tablet to her lap, and stared at him in acute dismay. "Oh, my God—have you told Acton this?"

Doyle blinked. "Aye, he knows."

Munoz bent her head, so that her hair fell in a curtain, on either side of her face, and then she brought her hands to the sides of her head. "Oh—I hate this feeling. I feel as though it's all my fault."

Doyle and Williams exchanged a surprised glance, and then Doyle asked gently, "How so, Izzy?"

Munoz took a breath, and then raised her face to theirs. "She came to speak to me—Yessenia did. She came to one of the community outreaches that I do for the Yard, and told me about her suspicions. She thought I'd be a good contact, since she could tell me about it in Spanish, which would help with the secrecy." Munoz paused, and then added a bit bleakly, "She was interested in becoming an LEO."

There was a small pause. "What were her suspicions?" asked Williams.

"She worked for New View Pharmacy, and she thought something underhanded had happened. The supervisor allowed some dodgy people on-site at closing time, and she believed unsecured product was added, to one of the deliveries. Then, when the company was rocked by the tainted-medication scandal, she decided she'd better say something to law enforcement, because her bosses were pretending it was strictly a quality-control problem."

Doyle stared in dismay. "Holy Mother, Munoz—what did you tell her?"

Munoz blew out a breath. "I told her to sit tight, and not to tell anyone else. Then I turned it over to Acton, and never heard anything further." She paused, and then whispered. "I can't believe she's dead."

With abject dismay, Doyle considered this ominous news, which seemed ominous in more ways than one—although she didn't want to raise it, in front of the others. Instead, she informed the other detective, "Geary was the SIO on Yessenia's homicide."

Munoz stared at her. "*Geary* was?"

"You didn't tell him, about Yessenia?"

She shook her head. "No—I followed the Whistleblower Protocol, and reported it only to Acton."

Into the silence, Williams said, "Well, someone else found out."

"Aye," Doyle affirmed. "We're guessin' that Yessenia knew that Enrique was the guard, on the delivery in question. She must have gone to speak with him, to try to find out what he knew about it."

"Maybe Enrique was the one who grassed her out," Munoz offered, in a subdued tone.

"Or, he started asking the wrong people his own questions," Williams suggested. "There's a reason the Whistleblower Protocol is so strict—the informant may be in real danger."

Munoz glanced at Doyle. "Acton didn't tell you—about Yessenia coming forward?"

"No," Doyle admitted.

"He has to be careful," Williams explained. "The wrong word in the wrong ear could disrupt the entire investigation."

"Or bring down massive disgrace on the Met, and make the public lose confidence," Doyle added. "That's part of his equation, even though sometimes I wish it weren't."

"It's a matter of priorities, Williams agreed. "There are no easy choices."

"And that's the difference betwixt the brass, and the foot soldiers, like us," she observed. "Acton's always more worried about the public's trust in the system, than he is about the outcome of any particular case."

Munoz bent her head. "I feel terrible. She would have made a good copper."

"We can't think we have to save everyone," Williams reminded her, reaching to touch her arm. "Just because you're the one she approached, you can't take personal responsibility."

They sat in silence for a moment, because this was something they drilled into you at the Crime Academy; law enforcement officers had to fight any feelings of personal remorse or frustration, when their efforts came up short. Harboring such feelings might affect their judgment in future cases—or encourage vigilantism; a lesson that had obviously sailed clear over Williams' head.

Munoz blew out a breath, and picked up her tablet again. "So, what's the assignment?"

"I'd better consult with Acton," Williams replied. "Take no further action—either one of you—until you hear from me."

"Yes, sir," said Munoz, who then turned to Doyle. "Want to go for coffee?"

But Doyle shook her head, as she took out her mobile. "Sorry—I have to pass. Today's my half-day, and I'm under strict orders to go home, and beach myself on the sofa."

"Tomorrow, then," said Munoz.

Faith, she wants to tell me something, thought Doyle, as she texted her husband. But I've got to address my first crisis first, and poor Munoz will have to wait in line, because my first crisis is a certain Chief Inspector, who's due for a brick-bat interrogation.

CHAPTER 25

He would have to tell her enough so that she would close this line of inquiry. A shame; she'd be disappointed in him, but he'd no choice. Above all, she must not discover the truth.

Doyle left Williams' office, and made her way over to the parking garage lifts. It seemed evident that she shouldn't confront her wayward husband on-site—the fewer witnesses, the better—and so, she'd texted him, and asked if he would mind driving her home, instead of the driving service.

He'd know immediately that he was in the soup, of course, but there was nothing for it; part of being a nob—with butlers and drivers and nannies constantly underfoot—meant you had to carve-out what privacy you could, and needs must, when the devil drives.

Not that he's the devil, Doyle quickly assured herself, as she smiled at a passing DC, who'd saluted her very respectfully. But this is one time that the gingerbread man is not going to be able to run away; not on my watch.

As she dawdled by the lifts, she contemplated the most alarming aspect of what had been revealed in the case-meeting —the part that she couldn't say, in front of the others. It appeared that as soon as Munoz told Acton about Yessenia-the-whistleblower, Yessenia-the-whistleblower had turned up dead. And nothing had been done—so far as she could tell—to bring what had happened to light, save for a chance encounter between Doyle, and the victim's mother.

And now—now, Yessenia's phone was missing from evidence when it shouldn't be, and Acton had asked Williams to lift the Met's surveillance tape of Doyle's interview with that self-same mother.

So—she had to face facts; as hard as it may be to believe, the situation had all the earmarks of an Acton cover-up, and— unfortunately—Doyle was well-familiar with those earmarks, having witnessed them in action, and on more than one occasion.

Of course, it was possible that everything was being covered-up because a sanctioned sting operation was underway—she'd got the feeling that Williams was hinting at this, during the meeting. And any sting would necessarily be a massive undertaking, since it was now known that the tainted-medication case and the Public Accounts case were linked— they'd have known it, ever since Yessenia came forward.

On the other hand, it seemed miles more likely to Doyle that her husband was manipulating matters to suit his own notion of what should happen, which was, after all, what he tended to do.

And—to be fair—his motives weren't necessarily bad ones, oftentimes. What she'd said to the others was true; Acton tended to protect the institution as a whole, rather than worry about who gets hurt by the fallout. In a way, it was similar to the "don't hold yourself accountable" mentality they were taught at the Crime Academy; Acton didn't weep, when good people were caught-up in the crossfire—instead, he tended to focus on the outcome of the battle.

Although there were definitely those occasions when it seemed to her that the outcome of the battle had a lot more to do with protecting the House of Acton, than protecting any public institution. As an excellent example, he'd covered-up her own shooting of Philippe Savoie's little brother, back in the day. And then there was Reynolds' plot to murder the Russian Colonel, which served as a far more recent case-in-point.

Her scalp prickled, and she imagined she knew why; the Russian Colonel's murder was the original reason that Blakney-the-ghost had told her to leave well enough alone, when he'd haunted her dreams. And now, he'd popped up again like a Jack-o'-the-clock, telling her to leave it alone, again—even though she didn't know heads-nor-tails about what was going on. She only knew that Acton seemed to be weaving his cover-up magic, yet again, although this time there were public institutions at stake, rather than a little Russian girl.

So; mayhap this would explain why Blakney was doing his second-act as a ghost; it was another situation like that first one, and he was urging her to trust Acton—after all, the ghost kept saying he had it well-in-hand, and that the fair Doyle should bow out, since women only tended to complicate things.

Although Blakney was another one, who held his own

notions of justice, and Doyle should not necessarily take his advice. The ghost was the sort of person who would roundly approve of the occasional righteous murder, whilst Doyle definitely would not. But at least she was now starting to get a glimmer of sense, out of the whole mish-mash.

Her husband's tall figure turned the corner in the hallway, and she smiled in a friendly fashion, just so that he wouldn't think it was a weapons-free situation. "Hallo, Michael—I'm sorry to pull you about; were you busy?"

"Never too busy for you," he said gallantly, and kissed her cheek. "How are you feeling?"

"The occasional cramp," she admitted. "Nothin' serious; now that I've done it before, I can tell."

They descended in the lift, and Doyle bided her time until they were enclosed in the car, and underway. Nothin' for it, she thought; the clock's ticking on the privacy meter, and I'd best get to it.

She began, "It's a rare crack, bein' married to you. It's amazin' my hair's not snow-white."

"This sounds ominous," he noted.

But she only frowned, perplexed. "I honestly can't understand, Michael; I always unearth whatever-it-is that you are tryin' to hide, and you'd think you'd finally learn that lesson, after the hundredth time."

There was a small pause, and then he said quietly, "A very good point."

She turned to him in bewilderment. "Can you not help yourself? Is it one of those 'compulsion' things, that they talk about with psych-cases? I'd like to help you, but I'm at a loss. I'd thought you were doin' so much better, lately."

She wasn't certain how he'd respond, because Acton didn't

like to talk about what was going on, inside that head of his. But in this instance, it seemed he was willing to engage in a discussion-of-sorts, because he replied, "You have been an immense help, Kathleen. I have been tempering my actions, in ways I would have never imagined."

This was true, and she observed, "That's because you used to think you'd nothin' to lose, and now you do."

"Yes—very well said."

She eyed him, sidelong. "But aside from that—and I do appreciate it, Michael; please don't think I don't—you also used to think that no one would ever hold you accountable. How it must rankle, that your dim-bulb wife is always pullin' the rug out."

"Not at all," he said graciously. "And you are not a dim-bulb, at all. I have always known that you are very clever—from our very first case together, in fact."

But Doyle recognized an attempt to steer the subject, when she heard one, and held firm. "Not so much clever, as on my mettle. I'm tasked with savin' you from yourself, Michael, and I'm not so sure that I'm doin' a very good job at it, since here we are, yet again."

Apparently, he'd determined that he was not going to be able to avoid his sorting-out, and so he turned the car onto a quieter side-street, and found a place to park, beneath some spreading tree branches.

He leaned back in his seat, and turned to take her hands in his. "You have done more than you will ever know, Kathleen. I had little hope of happiness, before I met you."

This seemed encouraging—he was being a good penitent, he was—and she gently teased, "Aye; and who could have foreseen such a thing? You used to be all scorched-earth, and now you've been hen-pecked into 'temperin' your actions'."

He smiled slightly, in acknowledgment. "It is very surprising, indeed."

But Doyle firmly quashed yet another attempt to steer the conversation toward more nostalgic topics, and said bluntly, "Tell me you are not committin' these containment-murders, husband."

"I am not," he said immediately.

Ruthlessly, she prompted, "Let's hear it."

"I did not kill Yessenia Moreno, nor Enrique Valdez, nor Rosanna Diaz. Nor did I arrange to have any of them killed."

She nodded, since this was true. It was somewhat of a relief, of course, but then again, she would have been very surprised if he *had* committed these murders; in a strange way, they were not his style—he didn't like to leave a trail of bloody corpses behind him, did Acton.

She frowned. "D'you know who did?"

"I have my suspicions," he admitted. "But there are other factors at play, and it is a delicate situation."

This was also true, and with no small exasperation, she chided, "For heaven's sake, Michael—people are gettin' themselves murdered, and if there's *anythin'* we can do to put a stop to it, we should do it, without fussin' about the 'other factors.' If there's a trap-and-seizure operation goin' forward, it's time to conclude it—arrest them, present whatever evidence you have, and let's be done with this."

He lifted his head, and gazed into the distance, out the windscreen. "All very true. However, I am in an unfortunate predicament, because I bear some responsibility for the Public Accounts skimming scheme."

CHAPTER 26

Careful, he reminded himself. Watch what you say.

*D*oyle stared at her husband for a long, horrified moment. *"Holy Mother,"* she breathed, when she could find her tongue. "Holy *Mother,* Michael."

"Yes. I am sorry, Kathleen."

Slowly, she turned to stare out the windscreen, alongside him. "I suppose I shouldn't be that surprised, truly. All that lovely money, washin' about, with naught but fat-cat bureaucrats, watchin' over it. So very temptin', for the likes of you."

"If it is any consolation, I was already in the process of extricating myself from the operation, before any of these murders occurred."

This was true, and she nodded. "All right—there's a ray of

hope, I suppose—more of that temperin'-business, goin' on."

They sat for a moment in silence, and then the penny dropped, and she turned to face him. "Charbonneau knows this—knows about your involvement?"

"I would imagine that she does. I am not certain."

Doyle blew out a breath. "So; *that's* why you've not rolled her up. But can't you clip her wings, somehow—send a message? She's murderin' people, Michael; you can't just stand back, and let her have at it. Besides, I'd be that surprised, if you haven't covered your tracks very thoroughly. Let her do her worst—even if she accused you, no one would believe it, anyway. Between the title, and your work at the CID, and your hero-wife, you're bulletproof."

She paused, realizing that this last statement was not worthy of an LEO, and so she quickly added, "But you'd still have to make amends; all the money you made should be given to charity—" she glanced at him "—a *real* charity—and you must promise me you'll put a stop to this sort of behavior. Promise me, on your honor, Michael."

"Readily," he said.

She eyed him. "Does that mean 'yes,' in aristo-speak?"

"It does."

She nodded. "All right, then; let's move forward—faith, but this marriage-business is a rare crack, and it's just as well that no one warns you when you're goin' in, all bright-eyed and bushy-tailed. How do we handle this?"

Slowly, he explained, "It must be handled very carefully, because if I seek any warrants, I believe there will be an attempt to pin these containment murders on me."

But she frowned at this, even though what he'd said was

true. "You'd only have the same immunity you always have, Michael—no one would believe it."

"Perhaps. I do have some concerns, however."

This was also true, and seemed a bit ominous—that the likes of him would be worried about what might happen. She sat in silence for a moment, dismayed and annoyed beyond measure that he'd done this to her again—she was sworn to uphold the law, but she'd a wayward husband who dabbled in major crimes, and she was pig-sick of being put into this sort of situation. And now—now it seemed he'd come a cropper, and there was a very real danger that the illustrious Chief Inspector would land himself in prison, with everything crashing down atop their heads.

Which seemed to indicate that the villains knew something that she didn't, and that her husband didn't want her to know —something ominous, like that sword, that was hanging on the thread over that Greek fellow, whatever his name was; Acton had told her once, but she'd forgot, because those Greek-people always had complicated names.

She paused, suddenly struck by the—the *wrongness* of this train of thought. She knew the man sitting beside her like the back of her hand, and there was no way *on earth* that he'd ever allow a bunch of desperate bureaucrats to back him into a corner; no way, no how. He'd pull the pillars down, before he'd allow the likes of them to hold the whip-hand over him—or the whip-sword, or whatever.

On the other hand, however, he had "concerns" and he was truly worried about them. Something was definitely causing him fits—he was that fashed, and drinking a' nights. There was something here that she didn't understand—an "ominous" puzzle-piece that she didn't yet grasp; one that he didn't want her to grasp.

Suddenly, an idea of what it might be came to her, and she asked, "Couldn't you enlist Savoie, to rein-in Charbonneau? Not to kill her," she hastily added, since this point may not have been clear. "But he must have some influence—she was workin' for him, in that prison skimmin' rig. I imagine he has some leverage that he could apply."

She watched carefully for his reaction, since it had occurred to her that the missing piece to the puzzle might be that Acton was trying to protect Savoie. After all, the two men were collaborating on various underworld projects, and she'd bet her teeth that one of those projects had been this Public Accounts skimming rig. Such a scheme called for foot-soldiers, and Acton was not one to command criminal foot-soldiers—Savoie was.

And it actually made a lot of sense, now that she thought about it; Acton could side-step any and all attempts to obtain leverage over him—faith, he could probably do it in his sleep—but he might have a tougher time extricating his partner-in-crime. Savoie was well-known as a criminal type, and he didn't have the protection of Acton's reputation and title—Acton was bulletproof, whilst Savoie definitely was not.

Not to mention that a ghost had once told her Acton was bound by a promise that he'd made to Savoie, being as the man had saved the fair Doyle's life. A promise of immunity, no doubt, and Acton was the type of nob to feel honor-bound, by such a promise.

So; there it was—Savoie must be knee-deep in this skimming rig, and it neatly explained why her husband was tied up in knots, about how he should move forward.

"I imagine Savoie does have leverage over Charbonneau," her husband replied, in answer to her question. "An excellent idea."

She made a wry mouth. "You don't have to humor me, Michael—I suppose you're already pullin' all available levers for stupid Savoie, and it just goes to show how complicated I've made your nice, orderly, law-breakin' life. In the before-times, you just had to worry about avoidin' prison all by yourself, but now you've got to worry about a whole cast of supportin' characters, who don't always behave as they ought."

"I am so sorry, Kathleen."

He reached to take her hands again, and she willingly clasped them, to show him that he was forgiven. "Tell me how I can help bring these horrid people to justice—d'you need me to listen-in to anyone?"

But he shook his head. "No. I know it may not appear so, Kathleen, but I do have matters well in hand."

Perplexed, she knit her brow, at hearing this particular phrase, yet again. "It surely doesn't look that way, from where I'm sittin', my friend. I know you're tryin' to decide the best way forward, but in the meantime, good people are gettin' themselves killed, including Nigel Howard—"

She paused, suddenly.

Into the stillness, he said immediately, "I did not kill Nigel Howard, nor did I arrange to have him killed."

"I knew that," she said. "Sorry—I shouldn't have even thought it."

"The fault is mine, that such a thought could be entertained at all."

But Doyle had been struck with yet another ominous

thought, and with some dismay, she guessed, "Are they tryin' to frame-up Savoie, for Howard's death? Is that what your 'other factor' is?"

Slowly, he shook his head. "No. I do not believe anyone is trying to frame Savoie."

Doyle thought she detected a little nuance, in his voice, but he was regarding her steadily, and so she decided she was being over-sensitive. Besides, on second thought, it wouldn't make much sense; if Charbonneau tried to frame-up Savoie, he'd only turn around and return the favor—Charbonneau was hip-deep in the prison operation, after all. Or even worse; Savoie was very handy with a long rifle, as they'd witnessed first-hand, in the Russian Colonel situation.

Her husband squeezed her hands. "Please don't worry, and again, accept my sincere apology."

Doyle nodded. "I'm glad you told me," she said, and—with a mighty effort—resisted the urge to rail at him a bit more; she shouldn't make him wish he hadn't been honest. And so, instead, she offered in a mild tone, "Don't forget your promise to me, Michael, and let this be a hard lesson learned."

"Indeed," he said, as he started up the car, and she was a bit surprised by the grimness, that lay beneath his mild tone.

CHAPTER 27

She'd come far too close—she was amazing, and he should never underestimate her. He should make certain she did not have opportunity to raise the subject with Savoie.

Doyle was yet again at the playground, despite Reynolds' best attempts to convince her to stay at home; she needed to go off into her alternate little world—where life was noisier, but simpler—so that she wouldn't dwell, too much, on her latest marital discussion.

One thing good, though; at least now she understood why Acton was behaving in a way that seemed so out-of-character. And it was no easy thing, for him to make that confession, so there was a tiny silver lining; he'd been forced to confess his sins, and because he'd been forced to confess his sins, she'd been able to extract a promise that he'd sin no more—at least, when it came to embezzlement schemes. Acton kept his promises, after all.

The playground was indeed noisy, with its usual cast of characters, and—despite having donned her tending-small-children hat—Doyle found herself dwelling on her discussion with Acton, with the niggling sense that it hadn't gone as well as it seemed to have gone.

Therefore, she willingly stepped back, when Reynolds insisted on pushing Edward on the swing—her swing-pushing days had come to an end, right around the eight-month mark—and instead, she retreated to sit on a bench, so as to think it over.

She lifted her face to the weak sunlight, and contemplated the swaying treetops, overhead. Acton was in a fix because he bore some responsibility for setting-up the very same skimming rig that he was investigating—or so he'd said.

But that excuse didn't wash—not really, because, after all, this was standard Acton-operating-procedure; if one of his rigs was involved in a reported crime, he'd make sure he was the SIO, so as to keep that unfortunate little fact from ever seeing the light of day. He was a past-master at smothering any potential problems in the crib, was Acton, and this one should be no different. Acton should be well-able to refute any and all accusations Charbonneau might bring-up against him—the man was a wizard, at throwing dust over his tracks—and he'd do exactly the same for Savoie, if needful—after all, Savoie had Acton-immunity.

And—lest she forget—she'd seen this principle in action, because, Williams had Acton-immunity, too. Williams had done a very foolish thing, once, but he'd been spared his comeuppance, due to his friendship with Doyle.

Ironic, it was, that the Williams episode had yet another Blakney tie-in. Williams had been sweet on Mary-the-nanny, at the time, and he'd inadvertently paved the way for Blakney, her husband, to be murdered. Acton had solved all problems, of course, but that little incident only served to prove her main point; Acton was as guileful as the day was long, and he was well-able to side-step any and all potential minefields, for himself as well as any others that he chose to protect.

So; he'd led her to believe that his hands were tied, due to Savoie's vulnerability, but that wouldn't wash—wouldn't wash at all. But, on the other hand, there was *something* that was making him wary, and upset—he'd been maladrome, he'd said, and had brought the problem upon himself.

Doyle's gaze fixed on Savoie, where he stood at his usual post. Mayhap the Frenchman knew what the issue was. After all, if he was the one who'd cooked-up the skimming-rig with Acton, he might be aware of whatever-it-was that had thrown a spanner in the works.

To this end, she called out, "Philippe; how's that baby breathin'?"

Willingly, Savoie walked over to speak with her. "*Bien*; she does not have the *haleter*, anymore."

"There you go; I think half the secret to raisin' children is knowin' when to wait it out, those times when they start doin' somethin' odd."

"*Oui*," he readily agreed. "There are many of the odd things."

She duly noted that Trenton had now shifted his position to be closer to her, and that Savoie—with a faint show of amusement—changed his own stance so as to not to allow his back to the other man.

Men; honestly, thought Doyle, who roundly ignored this posturing, and tried to decide how to casually bring-up felony-embezzlement, as a topic of conversation. "I hear you've taken my advice—about gettin' out of that prison rig—and good on you, Philippe. Very nasty people, involved in that one."

He seemed amused, and ducked his head. "*Oui*; I take your advice, little bird—it is good advice." With a gleam, he added, "I do not take Acton's advice, *toutfois*."

The last words held a nuance—a rather sharp edge, lying beneath them—and Doyle was startled by the burst of emotion that she could sense, beneath his casual manner. With a knit brow, she stared at him for a moment, nonplussed—Savoie rarely gave off bursts of emotion. "Oh—oh; did Acton gave you bad advice, then?"

"*Oui*," he replied, with a slight smile. "Bad advice."

Ah, Doyle thought; now I think I see—Acton must be trying to steer Savoie away from the shoals, in this Public Accounts mess, but Savoie doesn't want to follow his advice, for some reason—foolish man; he probably thinks he can brazen it out, or something.

And the last needful thing was to have hell-for-leather Savoie go to prison, because then the fair Doyle would be stuck raising hell-for-leather Emile, along with her own two sons, and such a scenario did not bear contemplation. Therefore, with all sincerity, she offered, "Acton gives good advice, Philippe—you have to give it to the man. You'd do well to listen to him, and stay well-away from the fallout."

The Frenchman cocked his head, in an admonitory manner. "The advice, I take my own."

"Can't argue with that," Doyle admitted fairly. "I'm much the same."

He seemed disinclined to discuss the matter further, and so Doyle decided that she'd best take a more direct approach, before he walked away. "D'you know what's happened to Charbonneau? Everyone's lookin' for her, but she's gone doggo."

"*Non*, I know not." He shrugged negligently, but it was not the truth.

Ah-ha, she thought; and there you have it—I'd a feeling, that Charbonneau was at the heart of this. Mayhap Savoie is trying to protect the wretched woman, whilst Acton wants to throw her to the wolves.

Making a show of shaking her head in disgust, she said, "Well, I truly hope they find her, and she finally gets her comeuppance; she's a nasty customer." In casual manner, she continued, "Charbonneau's a French name, isn't it? One of those ones that isn't spelled at all like it sounds—just like yours. Did you already know her, from your past?"

"*Oui*," he admitted readily, but offered nothing more.

It's like pulling teeth, she thought in annoyance; he's very like Acton, in that. She heard a ping, and saw Reynolds answer his mobile, pushing Edward with one hand, so that he could do so. It must be Acton, she realized; he's the only one Reynolds would respond to, whilst he was handling Edward.

Since her window of opportunity seemed to be closing down fast, she offered a bit hurriedly, "Well, let me give you some more advice, Philippe, whether wanted or unwanted; you should stay well-away from Charbonneau. I think she's trouble, and I think she's givin' Acton fits."

"*C'est vrai*," he readily agreed.

Suddenly reminded, she added, "D'you know how

Charbonneau met Reynolds? Seems a bit strange, that they'd know each other."

Savoie seemed heartily amused, and made to reply, but before he could, Reynolds approached her, Edward's hand firmly clasped in his, since the boy was loudly protesting this interruption of precious playground-time.

"Good afternoon, Mr. Savoie," the butler said politely. "I am sorry to interrupt, madam, but your doctor's appointment has been moved-up. Lord Acton requests that I escort you there— he will meet you, from work."

"Oh—oh, I'd forgot; it was supposed to be later on today. All right, then." She clambered to her feet, and firmly advised her unhappy son that he was going home, and there were no two ways about it.

It was just as well, she decided, as they gathered up their things, and headed out. She was getting nowhere, with her interrogation of Savoie, but hopefully, he'd take her warning to heart, so that Acton could move forward with whatever plan he was hatching. Savoie tended to listen to her, when all was said and done; he could be counted as yet another friend, in Doyle's small circle of them.

And then, there'd been that last bit, too; she was certain that Savoie did indeed know how Reynolds knew Charbonneau. He'd been just about to answer, when they were interrupted, and he'd seemed amused—although to be fair, Savoie always seemed amused. Except when he'd mentioned not taking Acton's advice, of course—she'd sensed a fair bit of animosity, beneath that statement.

So—if Savoie knew how Reynolds knew Charbonneau, it led to but one logical conclusion, and she'd been a crackin' knocker, not to have guessed it before now.

Pregnant-brain, she thought in annoyance; it has much to answer for.

CHAPTER 28

*O*nce Edward was safely stowed at home with Trenton, Reynolds drove Doyle over to Dr. Easton's offices, on Harley Street. Doyle hated going to the doctor with the heat of a million suns, but she decided she'd put it to good use, this time around, since she'd Reynolds sitting here beside her, as a captive audience.

"You know, Reynolds," she began. "I was just speakin' with Savoie about the Wexton Prison kerfuffle, and it made me wonder if it was Savoie, who'd introduced you to Charbonneau."

Immediately, the servant's anxiety level rose off the charts, and a bit flustered, he replied, "Oh—oh; perhaps it was—"

Bullseye, thought Doyle, although she only continued in a teasing tone, "Well, it only makes sense; I can't imagine that you rub elbows with dodgy prisoners in the normal course of things—unless you're some sort of criminal mastermind, in your secret life."

With a monumental attempt to recover his poise, the servant stammered, "I-I only met Ms. Charbonneau for a brief moment, madam, and I'm afraid I'm not at liberty to say—"

"All right, then," Doyle said, with a knowing air. "Don't tell me your secrets, my friend—even though I'll only believe the worst."

Reynolds was busy giving her some tale—he wasn't a very good liar, was Reynolds—but she had no need to listen, because she'd managed to confirm what she'd already guessed —the most likely intersection betwixt Savoie, and Reynolds, and shady-as-sin Charbonneau, would be the Russian Colonel's murder. The woman must have played some role in the scheme, being as she was affiliated with Savoie—mayhap she'd been a look-out, to signal when the Colonel was approaching the target area. Or mayhap she'd simply acted as a witness to Reynolds' participation in the plot—Savoie was one to make certain that he had multiple layers of protection; he hadn't survived this long, in his dangerous world, without being savvy about such things.

With a smile, she cut-off Reynolds' rather disjointed explanation. "Faith, Reynolds, I'm only teasin' you, and shame on me for pryin'. It's none o' my business, and I'll say no more."

But it was indeed her business—murder always was—and here was what looked to be a major piece to the stymied-Acton puzzle. Charbonneau knew that Reynolds was involved in the Colonel's murder, and she was using it as leverage, over Doyle's husband. Suddenly, it all made sense—it seemed clear that there was a war of leverage, going on, and that Charbonneau held a formidable trump card; small wonder, that Acton was at his wit's end—the last needful thing was for both

Reynolds and Savoie to wind up in prison, and thus leave her with three small boys—she'd be tempted to commit a major crime of her own, so as to join them there.

"Are you quite all right, madam?" Reynolds was viewing her sudden abstraction with a trace of alarm.

"Aye—I am. I was just—I was just struck by somethin', is all." As she contemplated the enormity of this latest disaster, she added a bit crossly, "You know, Reynolds, I'm always bein' called upon to be dreft, but I'm the least-dreft person imaginable."

The servant offered, "I believe you mean 'deft', madam."

"Oh—oh, 'deft', then. I'm at the bottom of the barrel, when it comes to 'deft', whilst Acton is at the tiptop—there's none defter."

"I believe you mean 'there is no one more deft,' madam."

Annoyed, she turned to stare at him. "Faith, that's what I just said, Reynolds—aren't you *listenin'*? Which brings up another point; Acton's up at the top, of the deft podium, and that means that he can't possibly be the gingerbread man—not a'tall."

Understandably at sea, the servant ventured, "The gingerbread man, madam?"

She explained, "Someone told me that Acton was like the gingerbread man, but that isn't true—that isn't true, at all. The gingerbread man came to a bad end, due to his undeftness."

"I believe you mean—never mind; as you say, madam." This, in a voice of resignation.

Doyle turned to review the passing scenery, mainly so she wouldn't gabble any more stray thoughts that happened to cross her mind—she'd best be careful, and think over this latest epiphany; think it through, and try to rein-in her usual impulse to run amok.

So; the elusive Charbonneau must know about the Colonel's assassination, and now she could lower the boom on Reynolds and Savoie, any time she so desired. And it would be an epic scandal, of course; the Home Office had been mortified that the CID wasn't able to solve the Russian man's death, and the discovery that one of Acton's minions had done it would be catastrophic—she wasn't sure even Acton could finesse such a disaster. Not to mention that Savoie had used one of Acton's rifles for the deed, just for insurance—for leverage, in the event the plot was ever found out. *Saints* and holy angels, in his own way, Savoie was just as wily as Acton.

I was that niggled, about our marital discussion, and I'd every right to be, she admitted to herself, with some annoyance. Yet again, I was led away, like a dog after a bone. I've been focused, all this time, on the Public Accounts scandal, when it was the Colonel's death scandal that was giving Acton fits. That's the reason he's been quashin' every bad deed done by Charbonneau, and refusing to hale her in front of the magistrates. The wretched woman's got a prime piece of leverage, over my husband—who ordinarily would just let the chips fall where they may; after all, he didn't have anything to do with the Colonel's death. But he can't let those chips fall, this time, because he wants to protect Reynolds, and he's sworn to protect Savoie—all because of me.

Brought up short, she added—and shame on me, for thinking it's only about me and mine; the main impact of such a scandal would land squarely on little Gemma.

Doyle wasn't certain that Mary's adoption of Gemma had gone through, as yet—it had been delayed, time after time, due to one bureaucratic error after another. So, imagine Mary's horror, if the assassination was exposed, and as a result, Gemma was whisked back to Russia, to serve as a political pawn for evil men. Not to mention that after the Colonel's death, Acton had been made a trustee for the girl—which wouldn't look well at all, if Reynolds' involvement in the murder-scheme was brought to light. All the more reason for the powers-that-be to send Gemma straight back to Russia, along with their sincere apologies.

That must be it, Doyle decided with a sinking heart; that's why Acton is feeling his way so carefully—and small wonder, that he was so very unhappy with Reynolds and Savoie at the time, for concocting such a plan behind his back. Faith, but things looked very grim, indeed.

Her scalp prickled, insistently, and she paused for a moment in surprise, before realizing exactly why it did.

It's because I'm on the wrong track, again, she realized. This theory doesn't make a lot of sense, mainly because I'm recalled to the one, shining truth that I know for absolute certain; Acton would never allow himself to be backed into a corner, like this—just the same as he wouldn't allow it to happen with the Public Accounts scandal. There was not the smallest chance that the bullet that had killed the Colonel could now be traced to his own weapon—manipulation of evidence was the man's specialty, after all. And, in a similar way, there was not the smallest chance that her husband hadn't concocted an air-tight alibi for both Reynolds and Savoie, at the Colonel's time-of-death.

And finally—although it pained her to admit it—if Charbonneau truly held any real leverage over Acton, the woman would simply disappear, never to be seen again. Doyle could name a few others, who'd suffered a similar fate.

And so, she was back to square-one; why was her take-no-prisoners husband allowing this turmoil to shake-up their lives? It was not like him at all—instead, he'd be ruthlessly efficient, in stamping out all fires, and keeping such stampings-out very quiet, so as not to upset his overly-pregnant wife. His overly-pregnant wife, who was fast putting two and two together, and coming up with some very alarming conclusions —after all, the last thing Acton would want is for the fair Doyle to have figured out even as much as she already had; the man might be trying to better himself, but she was under no illusions about what he'd do if anyone dared to cross him, or dared to try to back him into a corner. So; why wasn't he extricating himself from this increasingly tangled situation? What was giving the man fits?

Struck with a potential possibility, she turned to ask Reynolds, "Have you heard any news about my false Aunty?"

Reynolds admitted, "Ms. Wickham telephoned this morning, hoping to contact Miss Callie."

Doyle considered this. "You told Acton?"

"Of course, madam."

Doyle shrugged a shoulder, and turned to face forward again. "Well, Callie's been warned, so I'm not over-worried, on that front. I wish Acton would sort-out the wretched woman, and sooner rather than later."

"She does seem to be a pest, madam. It is all very unsettling."

And that, thought Doyle, is yet another strange occurrence; Acton's certainly not trying to protect Reynolds—or Savoie or Gemma—when it comes to my dear Aunty Wickham, but for some reason, he's allowing the woman to roam the city at large, even though he could probably roll her up without breaking a sweat. There are a dozen judges who'd gladly issue a restraining order, just on his say-so.

So; another strange puzzle. Could it be that her Aunty was *not* actually connected to Charbonneau? But surely, that would be a coincidence too far—that the blacklegs were frantically committing containment-murders and then—lo, and behold— her false Aunty appears, trying to winkle her way into Doyle's good graces.

But if she was indeed working for Charbonneau, it seemed to be a clumsy gambit—very undeft, it was, to think that the wily Chief Inspector wouldn't do a thorough background check on the woman, and note that her records had been scrubbed. Faith, it was a faint hope that the fair Doyle, herself, would fall for it—she'd be naturally suspicious of such a claim, which had only come to light after she'd managed to marry a wealthy aristocrat.

"I don't know—I can't help but think it's important, somehow," she mused aloud.

"What is, madam?"

"Why is my false Aunty doing this, Reynolds? She doesn't seem to fit in, with the rest of this leverage-war, that's underway. Neither Acton or me was goin' to fall for it—not for a hot second. We're hardened coppers, and not the sort of people who fall for a sob-story."

"Indeed, madam. I will say that I would be very suspicious of such a claim, myself."

She nodded thoughtfully. "Right; she doesn't fit in—not at all. It's a bit silly, compared to the other leverage, everyone's got—and there's some impressive leverage bein' applied, I must say. It's all rather like a wrestlin' match, where no one's budgin', despite the massive efforts being made. It's a stalebate."

"I believe you mean 'stalemate', madam," Reynolds suggested.

"Thank you, Reynolds," said Doyle. "You're a rare treat."

"It is my pleasure, madam."

CHAPTER 29

*D*oyle met her husband at the doctor's posh offices, but she didn't have a chance to settle into one of the posh chairs in the posh waiting-room, because they were immediately ushered into the examination room by a discreet nurse, who smiled warmly at Doyle.

"Thank you," said Acton, in a dismissive tone.

The nurse closed the door behind her, and Doyle eyed him, as she began to remove her clothes. "Faith, husband; I wish you were half so abrupt with my Aunty Wickham."

"Ms. Wickham is an annoyance," he agreed, as he helped her into her examination gown.

But Doyle was undeterred by his dismissive tone. "I hear she tried to contact Callie, again. How many attempts have to be made, before we can get a restrainin' order against her?"

But he pointed out, "A restraining order may only exacerbate the problem."

This was a valid concern, unfortunately; sometimes, when the civil court issued a restraining order to keep a harasser away, it had the opposite effect, and acted as a trigger—the harasser would only become enraged, and violent.

Which—ironically enough—is exactly what I was just talking about, with Savoie, Doyle thought. It's that "don't tell me what to do" attitude; if someone like Savoie had a restraining order issued against him, the first thing he'd do would be to violate it, just to demonstrate that no one pulls his strings. Acton, on the other hand, would pretend to obey it, but breach it all the same, and that was the main difference, twixt the two—Acton was as subtle as a serpent, and twice as guileful.

Which, of course, made it very unlikely that he was actually worried about her Aunty Wickham's possible reaction to a restraining order. With some doubt, she glanced at him, as he helped her step-up, to sit upon the examination table. "D'you truly think the woman's unhinged? It seems unlikely that she'd be the type to act out, if she's workin' at an Embassy."

"Here's Doctor Easton," he announced, as the physician came through the door.

Saved by the good doctor, thought Doyle—but don't think you're off the hook, husband; it was important that I find out how Reynolds knew Charbonneau, and now—now it's important that I find out why Acton is keeping his formidable mitts off of my Aunty. There must be a reason, that he's behaving so out-of-character.

Dr. Easton smiled, in his posh-doctor understated manner. "How do you feel, Lady Acton? Your husband tells me you are having a few pre-labor pains."

"I am," she agreed. "Here and there."

The man listened to the baby's heartbeat with the ultrasound device, and then nodded. "Sounds splendid; a big, healthy baby."

"His father's fault," she observed. "We Irish tend to be nimble little creatures."

He laughed, politely. "If you would prop-up your feet, Lady Acton, let's see how your cervix is doing."

I hate this, Doyle thought, as Acton helped her lay back, and she stared at the ceiling. You'd better be worth it, Tommy.

"Oh yes—you are at the end-stage, now, and it may be a good idea to induce labor. The perineum sustained some damage from the last birth, and it may be best to ensure that we can carefully control the process—"

"What's this?" Doyle interrupted in surprise.

"It might be a good idea, Kathleen," Acton offered.

The doctor continued, "Hold still; we'll break your water with a quick nip of the scalpel—"

But Doyle was already scrambling backwards up the table, on her hands and her heels. "You will stay back," she commanded the doctor, in her most authoritative police-officer voice; "You will stay back, or I will arrest you, here and now."

The startled doctor backed away, holding up his hands in submission, as Doyle slid off the table, wobbling a bit off-balance, in her haste.

"Kathleen; Kathleen, please—" Acton urged, reaching to steady her.

But Doyle wasn't having it, as she flinched away from him, and backed up against the wall, her chest heaving. "You will stay back, too; this was your idea, and don't you *dare* try to tell me it wasn't."

Stricken, her husband offered, "You've been so

uncomfortable, and I thought it might be for the best—" He took a tentative step closer.

"*Fan amach*," she commanded sharply, her face aflame.

Since it was never a good sign, when his wife began railing at him in Gaelic, Acton said to the doctor, "If you will excuse us, for a moment—"

"Certainly," said Dr. Easton, who beat a hasty retreat.

Acton turned back to his wife, but Doyle was already struggling into her clothes. "I'm goin' home."

"Forgive me, Kathleen—please."

"I can't trust you," she said, and firmly closed her lips for a moment, because her mouth had started trembling. "I can't trust you, Michael."

There was a long pause. "Please—allow me to drive you home."

"How do I know you're not plannin' another ambush?" With an impatient movement, she wiped the tears from her face, with the palm of her hand.

"I will take you straight home, my word of honor."

Since it would look very strange if she left without him, she drew a ragged breath, and nodded. In stiff silence, she walked by his side, out the private entrance and to the Range Rover, and she found—for the first time since they'd met—that she didn't want to look at him.

Count to ten, and take hold of yourself, lass, she self-scolded. You're in no shape to make a break for it, and after all, the man's your husband, and you love him—you'd love to brain him with a fire-jack, of course—but in the end, you do love him.

The silence continued until they were in the car and

underway, when Acton offered quietly, "Only tell me what I must do, and I will do it."

He was that wracked—which, of course, he should be—and so she began to say something that would ease his mind, a bit. But before she could form the words, she started sobbing, her chin to her chest, and unable to stop herself—her hormones were in a precarious state, and any little thing tended to set them off. Of course, this wasn't a little thing—not by a long shot. Her husband had schemed to whisk the fair Doyle out of the Area of Operations, because he knew she was fast figuring-out whatever-it-was he was trying to hide from her. Utterly miserable, she buried her face in her hands, and wept.

For the second time in two days, he looked for a quiet side street, and parked the car. Tentatively, he reached to draw her to him, and she went willingly, because—in the end—he was marvelously comforting, was Acton, and she couldn't seem to comfort herself.

She cried into his shirtfront for a few minutes, whilst he stroked her hair wordlessly. After the storm had passed, she sniffled, and said into his chest, "You will *never* try such a trick on me again."

"I promise," he said. "I am so very, very sorry."

She sat upright, still sniffling, and he passed her his handkerchief. "I would like to hear," she said, as she wiped her eyes, "why you felt it was necessary."

The dark brown eyes met hers, with a full measure of remorse. "I am afraid I cannot tell you."

"You can't, or you don't want to?" This was an important distinction, since it had occurred to her that there may be national security concerns, arising out of the Public Accounts investigation.

"I don't want to," he confessed.

She frowned, idly balling-up the handkerchief in her hand. "It must be a corker, then."

His chest rose and fell. "I am compelled to be discreet."

She glanced up at him. "Now, there's some aristo-speak, for you."

He smiled, slightly, and she could sense his profound relief, because it seemed safe to assume that divorce court was not necessarily looming on the horizon.

She blew a tendril of hair off her face. "It's hard to believe, Michael, that whatever-it-is, is worth—worth this."

"I would agree."

There was a small silence, whilst she came to grips with the unhappy fact that it seemed clear that he wasn't going to tell her. She ventured, "You did somethin' undeft, and now you're tryin' to repair the fallout, which is why you're lettin' certain persons—like my Aunty—run amok. There's pressure, being brought to bear, and you don't feel you can just strong-arm it away, in the usual manner."

"Something like that," he agreed.

She considered this, because this statement was not exactly true, and it was not exactly false. But one thing was certain; he was not about to unsnabble, anytime soon, and she was feeling like a damp wash-rag.

"I'm longin' to have a lie-down," she confessed.

Immediately, he turned to start the car. "We will go home. I am so sorry, Kathleen—you must know I did not take this step lightly."

"No," she agreed, as she smoothed her hair back. "Because after all, you're the walkin' example, of graveyard-love. You love me, somethin' fierce."

"I don't have to say," he offered gently, as he drove down the street. "Not to you."

CHAPTER 30

I *t was time to consider a concession, before any further damage could be done.*

Doyle went home, and since Edward was still napping, she proceeded into the bedroom with no further ado, and lowered herself into the luxurious comfort of the bed. She wasn't certain she could sleep—she was still that upset—but she wanted a bit of quiet, so as to sort through her rather jumbled thoughts.

Sleep came almost immediately, however, because she found herself facing Blakney, as she stood on the rocky outcropping, with the wind swirling about them.

"I'm that shocked," she confessed. "He truly wants me well-away from it."

"Exactly what I've been telling you," the ghost reminded her. "You're not needed, to muck it all about."

Frowning, Doyle disagreed. "I do think I'm needed, though,

Mr. Blakney. There's somethin' here's that's troublin' him. And it must be a crackin' corker, if he was willin' to go to such lengths."

"Keep your nose out," the ghost repeated. "He'll have to bend, sooner or later."

Doyle considered this. "Aye; I think there's a game of leverage goin' on, and so everythin's at a standstill. No one wants to be the first to blink, but no one's countin' the terrible cost."

Blakney sighed, as he crossed his muscled-and-tattooed arms. "That's always the way of it. The higher-ups—the guvs—try to one-up each other, while blokes like me just try to keep our heads down, so's we're not caught in the cross-fire."

Doyle offered, "I'm that sorry, that you were caught in the cross-fire."

He shrugged. "I wasn't one to toe the line, and it caught up with me, in the end—I didn't much like anyone's telling me what to do. So, in a way, I deserved it. Rosanna didn't, though —she was a sweetheart."

Her attention caught, Doyle ventured, "Rosanna, the graveyard-love victim? You knew her?"

He gave her a look. "A' course I did—took a tumble or two with her, since she was willing. I knew just about everybody, who worked the rigs."

Doyle blinked in surprise. "Is the bakery runnin' a rig? I can see a pawn shop doin' it—or a coin shop, but how does a bakery run a rig?"

He didn't reply, but instead lifted his chin, to boast, "Yeah— I made a nice bit o' dosh, running guns—although me and Mary had to lay low, due to having to hide Gemma." He paused, to lean over, and spit in contempt. "Fookin' Russians."

Doyle decided she may as well ask, even though it seemed that this particular ghost never wanted to answer any questions—faith, he never wanted to stay on-topic, either. "Is Charbonneau hidin' out at the bakery, then?"

The ghost sighed. "Haven't you been listening? You're to mind your own business, and leave well enough alone."

"That's not in my nature," Doyle admitted. "When I can feel the flutterin' wings, I've got to keep lookin', till I can see the birds."

He repeated with emphasis, "Go have your baby, little bird, and stay out of it. He's got everything well in hand."

But Doyle slowly shook her head. "But I don't think he does, Mr. Blakney, and you need look no further than the trick he tried to pull today—he's that worried I'll find somethin' out. He won't go after Charbonneau, and he won't go after Aunty Wickham. It's very unlike him."

But the ghost only raised his dark brows, and said, very seriously, "It's graveyard-love, so you've got to leave 'im be, or it will only get worse. Stay out of it."

At sea, Doyle ventured, "I was just kiddin' with Acton, when I said that. I'm one who likes to joke about."

"Well, it's no joke—he's not going to back down," the ghost emphasized. "He's not one to dance on anyone's string."

"Definitely," Doyle agreed with a whole heart. "But still and all, I've got to find the truth. Someone once told me—I forget who—that we should seek-out justice, even though the heavens may fall."

With a sound of impatience, he countered, "You have to remember, Miss Know-it-all, that there's the Crown's justice, and then there's real justice."

"Everybody can't decide to use their own yardstick," she insisted. "Else it will all fall to chaos."

"You're to stay out of it, and leave him be. He was a good guv, after that fookin' Russian got himself taken-down. Avenged my death, he did, and you can't ask for more than that." He chuckled, reminiscing. "Threw the bastard right overboard from one of the boats, as it was crossing the channel."

Doyle stared at him, and fast came to the conclusion that something was amiss, since Acton was the least-likely person to avenge a pawn-broker's murder, not to mention he wouldn't go to all the trouble of throwing anyone overboard; instead, a quiet transfer to Maghaberry Prison was Acton's revenge-of-choice.

Hesitantly, she ventured, "We may be speakin' at cross-purposes, Mr. Blakney; I've been talkin' about Acton."

The ghost lifted his brows in surprise. "Why would I want 'im to win? He's a copper."

Slowly, she realized, "You've been speakin' of Savoie. It was Savoie, who ran your rig, after Solonik got himself killed. You don't think Acton is the gingerbread man—you think Savoie is."

"Slippery as an eel," the ghost declared, with a great deal of admiration. "And he was a fair guv, too—he'd listen to blokes like me. You don't cross him, though." He lowered his head, and gazed at her with some significance.

Surprised, she protested; "I haven't crossed Savoie; instead, we're friends—well, sort-of friends. I killed his brother, though, and thank all available saints and holy angels he's never found out."

"See?" the ghost said, with a cocked brow. "Some things are best left alone."

"I will give you that point," she conceded.

"And you're not smart enough to cross 'im, in the first place."

This left one possibility, and Doyle blinked in surprise. "*Acton's* crossed Savoie?"

"He didn't mean to," the ghost explained fairly. "Thought he was doing 'im a favor." He snorted, softly. "I would have taken 'im up on the offer, in a heartbeat."

Slowly, Doyle shook her head. "I haven't the first clue what you're talkin' about."

"Exactly; stay back, and let it play out. He's the gingerbread man."

Doubtfully, Doyle ventured, "You know, Mr. Blakney, the gingerbread man gets outfoxed—and in the true sense of the word. The fox pretends to be all helpful, but then he winds up eatin' the gingerbread man, in the end."

The ghost stared at her in disbelief. "No—I don't remember that."

"Well, I'm an expert on the story, even though I'd rather not be."

The ghost scowled in annoyance. "Be that as it may, Miss Know-it-all, you're to keep your nose out."

And then Doyle found herself wide-awake, and staring at the ceiling.

CHAPTER 31

*D*oyle slid out of the bed, and went over to the mirror to make herself presentable for dinner. She paused for a moment to breathe-in the glorious scent that was wafting through the flat—Acton was on a contrition tour, which meant that he'd instructed Reynolds to bake her favorite shepherd's pie, with a crust that would be awash in lard. She wouldn't be able to eat much, of course—what with her stomach squashed up under her breastbone—but it was a sweet gesture, and much appreciated.

Thoughtfully, she gazed into the mirror for a moment, trying to make some sense out of the jumble of things that the ghost had spoken about.

He's a crackin' scatter-shot, she thought; it's as though there's a million spokes, all spinning around, but no hub—I've no idea what ties all these subjects together.

First and foremost, though, the ghost clearly admired Savoie—which was something of a surprise. And he'd said that

Acton had crossed Savoie—seemed fairly certain, on that point —but it made very little sense, because Savoie and Acton were partners-of-sorts; they'd formed an alliance, in their smuggling enterprises. Not to mention that Savoie was presumably in the soup, right alongside Acton, in this Public Accounts business. They would both have the same goal—to make sure Charbonneau and the crooked public officials didn't expose their own roles, in setting-up the skimming rig. Therefore, it didn't make much sense—that Acton would cross Savoie. Unless, mayhap, Acton was setting-up Savoie, as the fall-guy?

Almost immediately, she rejected this notion; Acton owed Savoie a debt of honor, and Acton would never double-cross him—not in a million years. It was one of those aristo-things, that was bred into his bones.

But—on the other hand—something was definitely giving Acton fits, so what was it? The ghost had said that pressure was being brought to bear, and this only validated her own sense—that her husband was engaged in a battle of leverage. But what was the end point of the battle—what was the goal? To stop the investigation? Little chance of that, with so many people now having knowledge of it. And there'd also been that reference to graveyard-love, which seemed significant— although what graveyard-love had to do with the Public Accounts skimming rig was a true puzzler.

Was Charbonneau in love with Acton? She wouldn't be the first, of course, but Doyle hadn't picked up that sense, when she'd met the woman in prison. Her Aunty? Was she in love with Acton? No—Doyle didn't have that sense there, either. So; who had a case of graveyard-love, where they were in it, to the death? It made no sense, in light of the facts on the ground.

And she mustn't forget an even more fundamental

question: Why had Blakney turned-up as the ghost, again? It seemed clear that he wasn't exactly on Acton's side—whatever Acton's side was. Blakney had been involved in the rigs, and he'd said Savoie was his guv, after Solonik was killed, but she wasn't sure why this mattered much, in the present crisis. He'd known Rosanna, the female victim—she was working the rigs, too—and, as a side note, it seemed clear he hadn't been very faithful to poor Mary. It was in keeping, of course; it always seemed to Doyle that the man loved Gemma, his little stepdaughter, miles more than he loved Mary, his wife.

She paused to consider this aspect, for a moment. Faith, when you thought about it, Blakney had a case of beyond-the-graveyard-love; he'd come to haunt the fair Doyle the last time, because he wanted to protect Gemma—even though he was no longer alive. He wanted Doyle to stay well-away from stopping the Reynolds-and-Savoie assassination plot, and in the end, he'd got his wish.

Reviewing her reflection, she knit her brow. *Could* it all be connected, somehow? Her ghosts always seemed to be relevant to something that was happening in her life, but try as she might, there seemed to be no rhyme nor reason, this time around. Blakney had no reason to fret, anymore—Gemma was safe and sound, under Acton's legal protection, and the Colonel's murder-case had gone cold. She hadn't even thought about Gemma's situation in a while; funny, that she hadn't heard word on whether the little girl's adoption had finally gone through.

With a thoughtful air, she made her way upstairs, to be greeted by a worried husband—she'd been so distracted by her dream, that she'd forgot she was angry at him.

He bent to kiss her, all a'fret, and probably checking to

make certain she wasn't carrying a suitcase. "How are you feeling?"

"Married," she said heavily. "Which is its own version of graveyard-love."

"I have your dinner ready, madam," Reynolds piped up, because he was always quick on the uptake, was Reynolds, and a fine judge of how things stood between the master and the mistress. "Shepherd's pie, your favorite."

"I'm that grateful, Reynolds," she said.

"Mum—I burnt my tongue," Edward advised, and showed her, for emphasis.

"That's always the danger, with shepherd's pie," Doyle agreed, as her husband waved Reynolds away, and saw her seated, himself. "It looks so delicious, but you have to be patient."

"I don't like the peas," the little boy confessed.

"We'll concentrate on the carrots, then—like a good little bunny."

"*The Runaway Bunny*," Edward exclaimed with delight.

Seizing the main chance, Doyle offered, "Say, let's read that story tonight—I've missed that one."

"No, mum; *The Gingerbread Man*," Edward insisted.

"There's always *Peter Rabbit*," Doyle countered. "He has to run away, too."

This gave Edward pause. "Both," he decided.

"Progress," said Doyle, in an aside to her husband, as she broke the crust of her pie with her fork.

"I've invited Callie for dinner, tomorrow," her husband advised, in keeping with his contrition tour.

"Good one; she needs a bit of support, just now." With a

glance at Reynolds in the kitchen, she lowered her voice. "Do we think she'll want to come-in tomorrow afternoon, to help with Edward? If she can't, I can work from home. Remember that Reynolds is goin' over to Mary's, for the homework sessions."

"I can ask the new nanny to fill-in tomorrow, if you would rather go in to headquarters," her husband suggested, because he was being all solicitous, and such.

"I'd like to meet this new nanny, and see how she handles our Edward, first," Doyle decided. "And it's no hardship, to work from home; I'm just an assist to Williams, after all, and probably more trouble than I'm not. I'll work in the mornin', and then I'll come home, and man the fort."

Edward protested the presence of peas in his pie, and so Doyle leaned over to fork them out, onto his plate.

Acton nodded. "Very good. Perhaps I should arrange for the new nanny to visit with you, soon." This, because Doyle was due to have a baby at any moment, but her husband dared not bring up this particular topic.

"Have her come along with us to the playground, tomorrow," Doyle suggested. "That's the true test of her mettle." Since Reynolds was refilling the water glasses, she added for his benefit, "Just ask Reynolds—it takes a stout-heart, and a keen mind."

But Reynolds only replied, "It is no trouble at all, madam," and this was semi-true.

She smiled to herself, because here was another one—like Savoie—who'd no idea that he was good with children, until he'd been pitchforked into it, will-he or nil-he.

And—on that subject—Doyle asked casually, as she continued her pea-winnowing duties, "Did Gemma ever get officially adopted? I remember it was always one stupid thing after another—the forms were wrong, and such."

Acton tilted his head. "I do not believe it has been completely finalized, as yet—mainly because I stand as one of her trustees. I would have been notified, if the adoption had gone through."

Oh-ho, thought Doyle, as she willingly granted Edward's request to transfer the objectionable peas onto her own plate, where he didn't have to look at them. Now, that was a direct hit, and my husband's on high alert, even though he's eating his stupid kale like there's nothing amiss. You have to admire the man; would that I had such a poker-face.

With a heartfelt sigh, she observed, "I hope what's happened to Howard doesn't affect it, at the last minute. It would only add insult to injury; poor Mary's been waitin' so long."

"We must be patient, I suppose."

And there it is, she thought, as she bent her head, to address her own pie—I think I'm finally on the right track. For some reason, Gemma's adoption is at the hub of this—whatever this is—that Blakney wants me well-away from. But even if that's what it is, it still doesn't make much sense; if the adoption has been stalled, why would Blakney want me to stay out of it? You'd think he'd be urging the fair Doyle to tie-up this particular loose end, so that there was no chance Gemma would be spirited back into stupid Russia, and their stupid political fights.

Not to mention there was an additional, troubling fact; Doyle had always suspicioned it was Acton, himself, who was holding up Gemma's adoption—he was the great-and-mighty Lord Acton, after all, and presumably could bring plenty of pressure to bear, so as to rush things through. But he wasn't doing it—although why the husband of her bosom wouldn't want Mary to adopt wee Gemma, and as quickly as possible, was a crackin' puzzler. What could it be? Since he stood as one of the girl's trustees, it wasn't as though he was afraid Mary would spend all her money, or something along those lines. It made no sense, whatsoever.

There's something here, she acknowledged; because Acton was like a hound to the point, when I brought up the subject. Unfortunately, I've no idea how to go about looking into it; I've no excuse—since it has no connection to law enforcement—and the last thing I'm going to do is quiz poor Mary on the subject, not to mention that I'm not exactly mobile, in the first place. So, I'm stymied, which—oddly enough—is exactly what the ghost wants, apparently. For some reason, the ghost thinks everything is well-in-hand, pressure is being brought to bear, and the fair Doyle should mind her own business.

"You missed this one," Edward complained, and Doyle leaned over to eat the pea off his fork.

CHAPTER 32

*T*he following morning, Doyle reported to Williams at his office, and was not very much surprised to discover that Williams had been given a stand-down order on the graveyard-love case.

"In light of the containment-murders, and their connection to the Public Accounts case, they want us to hold off, for fear we'll compromise their investigation."

"Who gave the stand-down order?" she asked, giving him a glance.

With a tinge of exasperation, he replied, "The Assistant DCI, Kath, and you have to admit, it only makes sense. Now they've got to build a case for murder, and if a conspiracy case is going to be brought against public officials, it has to be done very carefully."

"The Public Fraud Unit doesn't know how to handle homicides, though, we do."

"They'll make-up a joint task force, probably," he conceded. "But either way, we're on orders to hold."

Doyle blew out a breath. "We never got to speak to Mallory, at the tip-line."

He shrugged. "There's not a lot of reason, anymore. The crime scene was staged, and so we can guess that the tip was contrived, too. All signs point to Charbonneau."

"Aye," said Doyle thoughtfully. "Although if a CI is settin' up people for containment-murders, it would be mighty handy to have someone who mans the tip-line, as a cohort."

Williams leaned back in his chair, his hands behind his head, as he considered this. "Mallory would manufacture tips, to fit whatever was needed for the containment-murders?"

"Exactly. Not to mention that she'd be able to warn the blacklegs, if any honest tips came in, that might get them into trouble." Much struck, she paused. "Faith, that might be what happened to Yessenia."

"No, Yessenia spoke to Munoz, remember?"

"Oh—that's right. Where is Munoz?"

"She's coming."

Crossly, Doyle groused, "How come she doesn't have to be on-time?"

"Because I like her best."

She smiled, as he'd intended. "Sorry. It hardly matters—I've nothin' better to do, since now I'm without a case-assignment."

Williams confided, "I'm under strict instructions not to mention that you're in no shape to take-on another."

"Yes, well, we had a bit of a squabble on the subject, yesterday."

He shrugged a shoulder. "As a fellow-husband, I will only say that he wants what's best for you."

"I am well-able to figure out what is best for me, my friend."

With all good humor, he raised his hands. "All right—I'm not going to wade into it. But along those lines, did you quiz your driver, about your false aunt?"

"I did—on the way over, this mornin'. Hadn't the first clue what I was talkin' about."

"Good—although you know that Acton is going to be careful about someone he's put in that position."

"More than careful, Thomas; Adrian's another one—like your Lizzie—who springs from that town near Trestles."

He raised his brows. "Does he? That's interesting—she's never mentioned it."

"It's like a cult," Doyle pronounced. "They're all stuck in medieval times, and probably swear a blood-oath."

"I could see that," he joked.

"Aye, Lizzie's a fierce one—wouldn't want to be on her bad side."

But he shook his head, slightly. "She doesn't have any energy to go medieval on me, right now. I'm trying to get her to slow down, but she says she can't—not yet."

Doyle nodded in sympathy. "Well, we're tryin' out a new nanny, today, and so there's another pair of hands to help out, if she passes muster."

He gave her a look. "We can hope, I suppose, but in my experience, your nannies tend to bring the drama."

"Don't jinx it, Thomas," she begged. "And anyways, this one's a bit older, and so we can cross our fingers that she's well-past bringin' the drama."

"Unless she's Acton's sister," he teased. "Or his long-lost aunt."

"Don't be givin' my long-lost aunts to Acton, thank you very much."

He chuckled, and she teetered on the edge of asking him if he knew anything about Gemma's adoption, before deciding that she'd best not; Williams might say something to Acton, and it was important, for some reason, that Acton not be made aware that a tattooed ghost was holding forth, on that particular subject. Although the stupid ghost was yet another one, giving the fair Doyle a stand-down order.

"I think your tip-line idea has merit," Williams said thoughtfully, as he gazed out the window. "It should be looked into, anyway."

She reminded him, "If it's connected to the Public Accounts investigation, we've a stand-down order."

"I might do a bit of looking, anyway—just to see if I can find a pattern. If I think there's something there, I can pass it on."

She warned, "You are to hold off on any and all case-breakers, Thomas Williams, until I am back in action."

He laughed. "Of course, Kath—it wouldn't be any fun, without you."

CHAPTER 33

A knock on the door signaled that Munoz had arrived, and she entered to pull-up a chair, apologizing for being late.

"No worries, Munoz," Doyle offered, seeing that the other girl was unhappy. "We've been told to stand down, so there's little else to be done."

"I'm not surprised," the other young woman replied, a bit somberly. "I think information was getting leaked."

"Not by me," Doyle insisted, rather nettled, and trying to remember if she'd spoken too freely to anyone.

"No—I wasn't saying it was you, Doyle. But I put two and two together, yesterday, when I went to speak with Yessenia's mother—I felt so badly, about what had happened. She told me she'd heard gossip that Rosanna—the female victim, in the graveyard case, remember?—she'd been approached by Acton, and he'd offered her immunity, in exchange for her testimony against the others. She was going to grass them all out, but the next thing you know, she was a victim in this graveyard-love case."

There was a moment's silence, "Holy Mother," Doyle breathed. "How awful—poor Acton."

But her scalp was prickling, and when she paused to consider why it would, she realized the obvious—if Acton had set-up the skimming rig to begin with, he'd not need a grasser on the inside, since he'd already know everything there was to know. So—it must be that Acton was using Rosanna to run a misdirection play, so that she'd finger people who knew nothing about his own involvement—his or Savoie's. It was the only thing that made sense.

"You didn't know, about Rosanna's being an informant?" Munoz asked Doyle.

Doyle shook her head. "No. So, I can say, with a clear conscience, that I'm definitely not the leak."

"Obviously, someone is," Williams said. "Because all helpful witnesses are now dead."

There was a small silence, whilst they considered this rather bleak fact, and then Munoz observed, "I'd be furious, if I was Acton. You go to all the trouble to cultivate an informant, and then she says something to the wrong person, and winds up dead—not to mention that suspects are now aware that they've been twigged-out, and can start covering-up their tracks."

But Williams only said, "Acton doesn't get furious; he just recalibrates, and moves on. It's a hard lesson to learn, in this business, but it's a good one. You can't take anything personally."

"I suppose that's why he's the brass, and we're not," Munoz agreed.

But Doyle made no comment, being as she'd seen her

husband furious—and on more than one occasion. In fact, Acton's fury was a frightening thing to behold, but that little factor was probably not something she should share with present company; Acton had his mystique, after all, and it was half the reason he was a legend, around the Yard.

And—thinking along these lines—Doyle could only shake her head in disbelief. "I'm that amazed, that these paltry bureaucrats managed to outfox Acton. I met Charbonneau—spent some time with her, in fact—and she never struck me as bein' anywhere near so wily."

Munoz offered, "I imagine there's a hierarchy—like the mafia groups have—in order to set-up an operation this bold. The smart people are at the top, but they stay in the shadows, and out of the day-to-day operations."

Suddenly aware that she should probably steer the conversation away from the identities of the aforementioned smart-people-at-the-top, Doyle blurted out the next stray thought that crossed her mind. "D'you think they were runnin' a skimmin' rig, at Rosanna's bakery?"

Williams frowned slightly. "What do you mean?"

But Doyle decided that this thought wasn't so very stray, after all, and slowly reasoned, "It only makes sense—if Rosanna was going to grass to Acton, she must have been one of the players. And Munoz said that the bakery personnel were as dodgy as thieves in church."

"They were," Munoz agreed. "But I'm not sure how a bakery would be involved in skimming public funds."

Thoughtfully, Doyle offered, "Remember the horse-trailer rig—the one that smuggled illegal weapons? They used horse-trailers, because they could travel around to all the race-courses in the country, and no one would think twice. You'd think the same would apply to bakery trucks."

Munoz stared at her. "You know, Doyle, sometimes you have a decent hunch."

"I have decent hunches all the time," Doyle retorted, nettled. "And another thing; I'll bet my teeth that Rosanna's bakery supplied Wexton Prison."

Williams held up his hands. "Don't forget, we've been ordered to stand down."

"But if we come up with a good working-theory, you should pass it along," Munoz insisted. After struggling for a moment, she admitted, "I'd really like the case to be resolved, before Geary meets with Professional Standards."

"Geary's goin' up before Professional Standards?" Doyle asked in surprise.

Munoz nodded unhappily. "He handled Yessenia's case, and he closed it when he shouldn't have."

Doyle said stoutly, "We all know that Geary's not bent, Munoz; he's a good copper, and therefore he has nothin' to worry about."

"I know, but he doesn't want to talk about it." She pressed her hand to her forehead and confessed, "I'm so worried."

Slowly, Williams offered, "I will tell you something in confidence."

The two young women turned to him in surprise, and he continued, "Acton asked Geary to close the case, despite the inconsistencies. He didn't want the suspects to be made aware that their cover-up hadn't worked."

The words were chosen carefully, and Doyle's scalp prickled. Faith—that's what Williams knows, that he didn't want to tell me, she realized; Williams knows that Acton asked

Geary to close the case, and leave it be—and he probably also knows it was just as much out of self-preservation, as it was to protect a sting operation. Acton was running his own gambit with Rosanna, so as to make sure his name never came up—his and Savoie's—and Williams must have known all this.

Munoz nodded, much relieved. "Thank you for telling me —I won't say anything."

"Unless you're the leaker," Doyle observed fairly.

"I'm *not* the leaker, Doyle."

Before any escalation-of-arms could take place, Williams interrupted, "On a more positive note, I'd like to invite you both to Connor's baptism on Saturday, at ten."

Doyle smiled. "Oh—that's wonderful, Thomas. I'll be there —so long as I'm not busy, havin' a baby."

"Acton already said you'd be there—you're the godparents."

"How funny—he forgot to say," she said with an indulgent smile, and didn't add that he'd not said, because no doubt he thought he'd have the wife of his bosom safely stashed away with a new baby, and unable to attend.

"We'll be there," said Munoz. "Which church?"

He grinned at her. "St. Michael's."

Munoz raised her dark brows. "Really? You're baptizing him as an RC?"

"Feathers and beads," Doyle teased.

Williams held up his hands. "I am unashamed, although you two may have to hold up cue-cards."

"The power of love," Doyle observed. "I will say no more, although I never thought I'd see the day."

"Me neither," said Munoz. "So; no further action on the graveyard-love case?"

"No further action," Williams affirmed. "Everyone sits tight."

I'm sitting tight, even though I'd rather not be, Doyle thought, as she gathered her things to leave. The clock is counting down for little Tommy, and everyone—dead and alive —wants me out of the Area of Operations. It's almost a shame, that I've a niggling suspicion that I'll be needed, and soon.

CHAPTER 34

He felt he'd no choice, but to extend an invitation. He hoped Callie knew better than to speak about it, but she was not behaving rationally.

Callie's dinner was that evening, and Doyle insisted that it be a casual affair—nothing too formal, and they were to sit at the kitchen table, with Edward in his usual place.

"Callie is family, and we should treat her as such," she explained to Reynolds. "It's all a bit awkward, and so we've got to try and make her feel as comfortable as we can. Besides, there's nothin' like a cheeky toddler, to break the ice."

"Very good, madam," said Reynolds, who kept his opinion to himself. It was interesting to Doyle that—despite Callie's connection to the House of Acton—Reynolds was still a bit disapproving of the girl. He supports the nobs, as long as the nobs behave in a worthy way, she surmised. He doesn't much like the way Callie's been shirking her obligations, lately.

When the appointed time came, they discovered that Melinda, the girl's mother, had invited herself, and Doyle suppressed a pang of disappointment, because she felt it would have been miles more comfortable to deal with Callie alone. Melinda tended to be a wild-card, and say whatever she felt.

"Acton," Melinda said, and kissed his cheek, in her negligent manner. "Many, many thanks, for steering me toward Sir Vikili's colleague."

Surprised, Doyle asked, "Are you seein' someone, Melinda?"

The other woman laughed, as Reynolds took her coat. "No—not at all; I'm concentrating on Callie, right now. But my late husband's mother has solicitors who send me scolding letters, and so I asked Acton for the name of someone who could scold them right back."

"Oh," said Doyle, who saw this topic as a clear example of exactly why she wished Melinda hadn't come. "Well, if he's someone Sir Vikili recommended, he'll have plenty of teeth." Sir Vikili was a rather notorious barrister, known for getting wealthy blacklegs off the judicial hook.

"She," Melinda corrected. "A lady-solicitor, who nevertheless does look to have plenty of teeth." She said in an aside, to Reynolds, "My mother-in-law is Lady Madeline. A thoroughly detestable woman."

"I have met the lady, on the telephone," Reynolds confessed.

"Have you?" Melinda's thin brows rose. "Don't listen to a thing she says, Reynolds; she's a gorgon—thinks I'm a trollop."

"May I offer a glass of wine?" the servant offered hastily.

"Callie, would you care for wine?" Acton asked, in a polite tone.

"Oh—yes, that would be lovely."

"Me, too," said Melinda easily.

"Splendid; we have a fine chardonnay," Reynolds said, as he courteously ushered Callie into the sitting room area, with Melinda following.

No need to rebuke him twice, thought Doyle; Reynolds is very fast on his feet.

The pre-dinner conversation was necessarily curtailed a bit, because Edward was hungry, and not ashamed to let everyone hear about it.

"It's pasta," he told Callie. "With white sauce. There's no peas."

"Good; I don't care for peas, either," the girl admitted.

"Will you sit next to me?"

"Of course, I will."

"Edward," said Doyle. "You mustn't hang on Miss Callie; come over and sit with me, please."

But the girl only shook her head, her gaze on the child, as she ran a hand over his head. "That's all right, Lady Acton; I don't mind."

"Kathleen," Doyle reminded her gently.

"Kathleen," Callie offered, with a tight smile.

Faith, this is crackin' awkward, Doyle thought. She's a bundle of resentment, is our Callie.

Fortunately, Edward was oblivious to any and all cross-currents, and announced to her, "I have a new boat, for the bath. Mr. Reynolds says it's a tug."

"Miss Callie's a guest, tonight, Edward," Doyle reminded him. "She's just visitin' us, for dinner." Little hope of trying to explain the niceties of a nanny-turned-aunt to the little boy; Doyle could barely navigate that maze, herself.

"No worries, Edward; I'd love to give you a bath," the girl replied, and for the first time, Doyle thought she saw the glimmer of a genuine smile.

"There's only one boat," the boy confessed.

"We will take turns, then."

"She will make a wonderful mother, won't she?" Melinda pronounced, as she watched this interaction with a fond smile.

Oh-oh, Doyle thought; not the best topic for Melinda to bring up. With a show of warmth, Doyle offered, "Edward does love our Callie—all the way back from our stay at Trestles."

"Is that so? I wouldn't know—I was barred from Trestles." This, said with all good humor.

"You still are," Acton offered, with his own show of good humor.

"Dinner is served," Reynolds hastily announced. "If you would please take your seats?"

The interruption served to break some of the tension, and they all moved to the kitchen table—a bit crowded, since Reynolds had squeezed-in an extra place for Melinda.

As they began the meal, Doyle asked, "How are your parents in Meryton, Callie?" She'd decided it would be best not to completely ignore the massive elephant in the room.

But this attempt was apparently ill-advised. "They are doing well," said Callie, in the tone of someone who doesn't wish to speak about it.

"Lovely people," Melinda pronounced. "A bit bewildered, of course. We're having a tug-of-war, as to where Callie should live."

Hurriedly, Doyle offered, "It must be nice, to be in such demand."

Callie did not respond, but Melinda said, "I'm looking to buy a property, outside of London. Could you point me toward a decent real estate agent, Acton?"

Acton said in a neutral tone, "Certainly. Although it may be best to wait until the estate is settled."

"I have every confidence," Melinda declared. "Now that I've my lady-solicitor."

"I saw a ladybird," Edward piped up, trying to be part of the conversation.

"Yes—today," Callie said. "It was lucky, that she landed on you—it's good luck."

"I wanted to keep her, but Callie said she has her own house."

"Exactly," Doyle agreed. "Can't be kidnappin' ladybirds— they'll send the ladybird police out, to arrest you."

Edward giggled, whilst Melinda declared in fulsome tones, "Oh—I can't *wait* to be a grandmother."

Noting the way Callie pressed her lips together, Doyle gently chided, "It's early days, yet, Melinda."

"Maybe not," the other woman said, a bit archly. "I think Callie already has someone in her sights."

Callie kept her gaze on her plate, and made no reply. Whilst Doyle frantically tried to think of a way to divert the conversation, her husband came to the rescue. "You mustn't pry, Melinda. It would be a case of the pot and the kettle."

Melinda laughed, as he'd intended—since she was not someone to take offense—but Doyle noted that Callie had lifted her sullen gaze to Acton, for a quick moment.

Oh-oh, thought Doyle; what's this? She's resentful, for some reason. Mayhap Acton warned her away from Savoie—which would be well-done of him, after all. Or mayhap he's given her a lecture about the many chousers who would be interested in Lord Acton's sister for all the wrong reasons—that seems even more likely. And it probably didn't go well, because neither one of them would know how to have such a conversation without pulling caps—faith, but this 'relatives' business is a crackin' minefield.

Edward, however, was oblivious to any and all minefields. "Are you coming to the playground tomorrow, Callie?"

"Miss Callie," Reynolds corrected, from the kitchen.

"Aunty Callie," Doyle corrected, in turn.

"Oh," the little boy said, reminded. "Aunty Callie. You're my aunty, now; that's what mum says."

Softening, Callie paused to address the little boy. "I suppose I am, Edward. It's all a bit confusing, isn't it?"

"You can never have too many relatives," Doyle declared, in an overly-hearty tone.

But now it was Doyle's turn, to be on the receiving end of a flash of resentment, as Callie pointed out, "You can't really say anything; you don't want to see your own Aunty, after all."

Doyle blinked, and Acton said immediately, "We've spoken about this, Callie."

Oh-oh, thought Doyle; Acton's in rebuking-mode, which does not bode well—obviously, he was hoping I'd not hear about this.

Mulishly, the girl continued, "It doesn't seem fair—you should at least give her a chance."

"What's this?" asked Melinda in bewilderment.

Nothin' for it, thought Doyle, who explained, "There's a

woman who's come 'round, claimin' she's my long-lost aunt. But it looks to be a fish-tale."

"Why couldn't it be true?" Callie protested. "And she's longing just to be given a chance." The girl then glanced at Melinda. "I had no idea about you, after all."

Since this last comment was said with a tinge of bitterness, Doyle hastily offered, "But Acton's looked into it, Callie—really dug deep—and he couldn't find any connection between this woman and my mother."

"Indeed," Acton agreed, in the tone of someone who's already gone over this ground, and was not happy to have to do it again.

"A grifter," Melinda pronounced, holding her wineglass in a languid hand, and completely unaware of the irony, lying thick on the ground.

It seemed clear that Callie was winding up to make a heated remark, and so Acton curtailed her in a quiet tone, "Let's say no more on the subject, please."

"We have a soufflé, for dessert," Reynolds quickly announced.

"I helped," Edward piped up. I beat the eggs, with the wisp."

"Brilliant," Callie said, and struggled to smile at him.

"I've never managed a soufflé," said Melinda, in an indulgent tone. "And I wouldn't know which end of a wisp to use."

"I dropped it in," Edward confessed. "But Mr. Reynolds said not to say."

"It was quite clean," Reynolds hastily interjected, and then, because he couldn't help it, added, "The *wisk* was quite clean."

"Oh, this is delicious," said Doyle brightly, even though

she'd burnt her tongue, in her haste to shift the topic. "Well done, to the both of you."

But Edward had been struck with an idea, and turned to Callie, "Can I bring the wisp into the bath?"

Doyle—having read her husband's mood aright—interrupted in a cheerful tone, "I'll bathe you tonight, Edward —I insist. And we'll bring-in the wisp, along with the sauce-strainer, for good measure."

"Then I think I'll go," Callie announced, rather abruptly. "I'm quite tired."

Melinda blinked at her daughter in surprise. "Is there any chance I could have one more glass of wine?"

"No," said Callie baldly, as she rose, her cheeks flushed.

There was a tense moment, whilst Edward regarded Callie with wide eyes. "Can I have your soufflé?"

"You may," the girl replied, in a softer tone, and then leaned to kiss him. "Goodbye, Edward—I will see you Monday."

Their visitors took their leave, Acton's manners impeccably polite, as he escorted them to the door. Doyle was not fooled, however, and said, in an aside to Reynolds, "Is the liquor cabinet stocked?"

"It is, madam," the butler replied, wooden-faced.

Doyle blew out a breath. "Well, that was a bit ragged, but at least now the ice has been broken, and it will be miles less awkward, next time."

"I am certain of it, madam," Reynolds soothed, and this was not at all true.

CHAPTER 35

$\mathcal{T}$he next day was the baptism at St. Michael's Church, and Doyle dutifully stood as little Connor's godmother, wishing that the only dress that still fit was not the stupid plaid one, that she'd worn at Christmas—it made her look like a tartan picnic table, but she hadn't any time to go shop for another, and it seemed a bit silly to buy a new tent-dress for only the one occasion.

It was an intimate gathering, with only Williams' relatives and a few friends from work in attendance, and afterwards there was punch and cake, in the reception hall.

One of the benefits to being the size of a walrus was that no one expected you to mingle and chit-chat, and so, with some relief, Doyle sat on a chair against the wall, watching the other guests, and sipping her punch.

"Any day, now?" Nellie, the Filipino woman who acted as Father John's strength and salvation, paused to speak to Doyle, even though she couldn't tarry too long; she ran these events with the precision of a railway conductor—not to mention that she was probably extra-wary, with this bunch, if she remembered what happened the last time some of Scotland Yard's finest attended a sacrament.

Doyle replied, "Any day—thanks be to God."

Nellie, who'd birthed nine, smiled in sympathy. "Only look ahead—we'll be back here for another baptism, before you know it."

"Aye, we will; and if you need to winkle anythin' from Acton for the church, now's the time."

Nellie laughed. "There is nothing I can think of, Kathleen. Did you know that I have a paid position, now? I've an office, and we've hired a bookkeeper."

With a smile, Doyle gazed around the reception room. "Faith—d'you remember the olden days, with the boiler that always broke down, so that we had to wear our mufflers and coats, during Mass? It's a shrine-worthy miracle that this place is so fine, now."

Nellie nodded, as she ran an assessing eye over the room, and then turned to Doyle, again. "Did you meet Ms. Wickham, the Irishwoman?"

"I did," said Doyle, and then offered nothing further, which was very unlike her.

Nellie nodded wisely. "I thought as much; I told Father that I thought she was asking too many questions about you—but you know how he is."

"I do, indeed. Lucky, he is, that's he's got suspicious women, about."

Nellie laughed again, and then left to make her rounds, whilst Munoz wandered over to take her place.

Since the other girl seemed distracted—too distracted to

even say hallo—Doyle ventured cautiously, "What's wrong, Munoz? You're as glum as a pilgrim at Lent."

"Nothing," said Munoz, her gaze resting on Acton, Williams and Geary, who were discussing something in low tones.

Taking a good guess, Doyle offered, "If Acton is runnin' interference for Geary, Professional Standards won't lay a finger on the man—you must know this."

"No—I know. That's not it."

There was a long pause, and then Doyle let out an exasperated breath. "Well, tell me or don't tell me—I don't much care. I'm not much interested in playin' twenty-questions, either."

Munoz bent her head forward, and pressed her fingers against her temples. "If Lizzie Williams is pregnant before I am, I will scream."

Agog, Doyle stared at her. "Lizzie is *pregnant?*"

"She was throwing up, in the loo."

"*Holy* Mother. Don't say anythin'—Williams may not know." This was an educated guess, being as the man already had his hands full with the first surprise-baby.

Munoz raised her head, and took a breath. "I know I shouldn't be resentful, but that only makes me feel even worse. What is *wrong* with me?"

But Doyle wasn't having it, and scolded, "For heaven's *sake*, Munoz; nothin' is wrong with you—there's a baby floatin' about in the universe, and she's headed your way on her own timetable—there's no rushin' her. So, stop bein such a baby, yourself."

This evoked a small smile. "How do you know it's a girl, Doyle?"

But Doyle firmly declared, "It's a girl, and you're goin' to name her Yessenia, because you'll want her to be strong, and brave."

Munoz broke into a chuckle. "I have to hand it to you—you say it with such confidence."

Best button my lip, Doyle thought.

Father John came over to greet them, and said in a hearty tone to Munoz, "I'll be ready for yours next, lass."

Inwardly, Doyle winced, and hastily offered, "Now, Father, it's early days. You just want to pad the rolls."

"Anything for the church," Munoz joked, and then her husband came over to retrieve her, and she bade them goodbye.

Father John stood beside Doyle for a few moments, watching, as Williams' and Lizzie's families assembled to take photographs together.

"And, speakin' of paddin' the rolls," Doyle teased, "there's a couple more parishioners, caught-up in your toils."

"I'm not certain if either one of them has heard the call," the priest admitted. "But God works in mysterious ways."

"Don't I know it. And you should give me a finder's fee, Father. I keep herdin' new recruits, in your direction."

"Aye," the priest agreed amiably. "And there's Mary's new beau, too."

At sea, Doyle asked, "Who's 'Mary'?"

Father John looked down at her. "Why, Mary Howard, lass."

Doyle blinked. *"Mary Howard has a new beau?"*

But she discovered that Father John was regarding her with equal surprise. "Aye—that French fellow."

The penny dropped, and Doyle smiled. "Oh—oh, Savoie,

you mean. That's right, he brings her over, for Mass. But he's just a friend, Father; mainly, I think he's terrified she'll move to Leeds—his son and her daughter are fast-friends."

Father John regarded her with a twinkle. "The man's sweet on her."

Astonished, Doyle could only stare. "*Savoie* is sweet on *Mary*?"

"Don't doubt me, child." With an air of satisfaction, the priest clasped his hands behind his back, and rocked on his heels. "He'll be a welcome addition, when she's done with her mournin'." He then leaned over to confide, "I think he's well-to-do; he's already given me a fine check, for the endowment fund."

"Oh; oh, well, that's grand, then."

Doyle lapsed into silence, not certain why she found this so unsettling, even though she did. Come to think of it, she remembered hearing that Trenton and Savoie had nearly come to blows, once, when Mary had been in need of some protection—but she'd put that down to two alpha-males, each vying to manage the situation. It had never occurred to her that Savoie might harbor warm feelings for Mary—mainly because she'd seen Savoie in action with Munoz, back when she was single, and he wasn't the type to patiently wait around for some woman to notice him.

Faith, it would be the eighth wonder of the world, if Savoie was methodically getting his ducks in a row with Mary, throughout all this misery and turmoil. Doyle was almost certain Mary had no idea, if such was the case—now, there would be deftness, in spades. But it just didn't seem in keeping, to her; deftness wasn't really Savoie's style—he was more of a sharp-elbows-and-bull-rush sort of person.

She was still distracted by this revelation, when Acton approached, to bid goodbye to Father John, and to gather-up his wife. "Shall we go home?"

He was being careful not to do any orderings-about, which was much appreciated; mayhap the shameful scene at Dr. Easton's had a silver lining. "We shall. I'm that ready for a nap."

He helped her to her feet, and as soon as they'd left out the portico, she told him in a low tone, "Wait until you hear this, Michael—Father John thinks Savioie is sweet on Mary Howard, of all people."

"Does he?"

With some surprise, she glanced up at him. "You're not over-shocked, husband. Has everyone noticed this, but me? I must be losin' my touch—I'm usually a noticer like no other."

"I did wonder," he admitted. "I thought it best not to say anything."

Frowning, she brought her gaze back to the pavement ahead. "Fancy that—I've had pregnant-brain, I guess—not to mention that's the last thing you'd think, to put those two together. But it makes me uneasy, Michael; do you think Charbonneau knows he's fond of her? What if she tries to pin Howard's murder on Savoie, as another way to bring the both of you to heel?"

"Charbonneau is certainly capable of such a thing," he agreed.

She glanced at him in alarm. "Well, we can't allow it, Michael."

Acton paused for a moment at the car, as he considered what to say. "I am confident that Savoie will not take the fall for Howard's death."

As he helped her into the passenger seat, she noted with some surprise, "You're all conflicted about this, husband. You can't be wishin' for Savoie to wind-up in prison—can you?" Remembering her earlier suspicion, she added, "Unless— unless that's what would help you out of this Public Accounts mess—havin' Savoie take the fall."

His chest rose and fell, and he paused, before closing the door. "I must carefully consider all options. There are times when we must be content with the least-worst solution."

She nodded, a bit taken aback that he would be worried enough to consider such a solution—the situation must be miles more grim, than he'd let on.

Slowly, she shook her head. "I don't know, Michael, I know you're takin' a lot of other factors into account—important ones —but we can't just let Charbonneau get away with everything; she's due for a hard dose of justice, same as all the blacklegs on the Commission. They're murderin' people, just to protect their reputations, and it would be the worst-worst solution, if we let her get clean away with it, or if we let Savoie get framed-up, just so as to protect your own reputation."

Quietly, he asked, "What would you have me do?"

This, of course, was an excellent question, being as the husband of her bosom seemed to think that he might be facing some prison-time, himself, if he went hard after Charbonneau. And the fallout from such a downfall would be vast and far-reaching; it was entirely possible that every case Acton had ever closed-up—and there were many—might have to be re-opened, if the public began to suspect that he was corrupt. It would be a massive fall from grace, and there would be plenty of blacklegs—like those on the Commission—who'd be only too happy to bring him down.

Reluctantly, she admitted, "I should say, 'let justice be done, though the heavens fall', but I'm not sure I can. The heavens would fall down with a crackin' vengeance."

He nodded. "Yes. I am not certain that would be best-case."

Making a wry mouth, she observed, "And I don't know if Savoie would stand bluff, and take the fall, in the first place— he's not like you, with debts of honor, and such."

"I would agree with your assessment."

She sighed. "Small wonder, that you're conflicted."

But he only assured her, "All will be well, Kathleen. My promise on it."

"I know," she said, and reached to take his hand. "I know— you're tryin' to decide the least-worst way forward, and I don't envy you. But I do hope you've learned a lesson, from peerin' over into the abyss, like this. You can't take such risks anymore, Michael."

"I agree completely," he said, and carefully shut the door.

CHAPTER 36

*S*avoie *had gone quiet. Perhaps he would reconsider, and change his plans. He was at a disadvantage, because he was powerless, with respect to the girl's future. He'd be foolish to risk it.*

The following Monday saw Doyle working from home—compiling hideously boring statistics—and so she decided to leave it aside for an hour, so as to rest her poor non-numbers-oriented brain, whilst Edward took his nap.

She'd been asleep for a small space of time, when her phone buzzed—which was an unusual occurrence, since Acton usually texted, first, to make certain she was awake before he called.

She reached to check the ID, and saw that it was Adrian. Pausing for a moment, she tried to remember if she'd forgot that he was supposed to drive her somewhere.

No, she decided; and curious, she pressed him on. "Ho, Adrian."

"Hello, Lady Acton; I am sorry to disturb you, but I thought I'd better call, just to check. It seemed unusual that Mr. Trenton didn't accompany Edward."

Suddenly wide-awake, Doyle swung her legs over the side of the bed. "Where is Edward? Is he with you?"

"Callie asked if I would drive them over to Mrs. Howard's flat, to visit with Gemma and Emile."

"Oh." Doyle took a breath, and dialed down her panic. "And Trenton didn't go with them?"

"No ma'am. I tried to call him, just now, but he didn't pick up."

With a knit brow, Doyle checked the time. "Well, there's a wrinkle; Edward should be nappin' down the hall from me."

"I dropped them off, about ten minutes ago."

Making a decision, Doyle asked, "Can you come fetch me? I'll go over, too."

"Right; I'm almost back at the building."

"Let's not mention this to anyone else," she said lightly.

"Right," he replied, in a neutral tone.

She rang off, and thought, he knows Callie's not following Acton's security protocol, and he doesn't want her to get in trouble, just as much as I don't. Although Acton can't very well sack his own sister, I suppose.

She paused, and decided that this was, in fact, entirely possible, and so she hurriedly pulled-on her coat, and tiptoed to the front door, to let herself out—although there was no need to tiptoe, she reminded herself. There was no one else here; Reynolds was over at Mary's, and Edward and Callie had flown the coop. Which—come to think of it—might be why

Callie thought Trenton wasn't needed—between Adrian and Reynolds, there would be security aplenty. But it did seem odd that Trenton hadn't picked up—mayhap he was napping, too.

But she had to admit, as she watched through the lobby's window for her ride to arrive, that Adrian was right; it was odd that Callie would take Edward somewhere without checking-in, first—even though Doyle was asleep, and Reynolds was not at home. If she couldn't get permission, she would have no choice but to stay home—Acton was very strict, about such things.

Although—mayhap the girl got permission from Acton, himself, Doyle realized, and pulled her phone to check-in with her husband. But her thumb hovered over the button without pressing it, and then she put the phone down again. Acton would never tell Callie she could take Edward anywhere without Trenton, she decided. Which makes this little excursion all the more puzzling.

Adrian pulled up, and as he came around to open the door, Doyle suddenly realized that there might be an obvious reason for Callie's excursion; it might be that the girl was looking for an excuse to speak with Savoie, and taking Edward over to Mary's would serve as a plausible excuse—Reynolds would be busy helping with homework, and Mary would be napping with the baby. Callie had been asking when the new nanny started, and this may have been the reason—the days were winding down for her to go plead her case to Savoie, in the guise of bringing Edward over for a visit.

Poor, silly thing, Doyle thought, with exasperated sympathy. The last person who'd appreciate an unsolicited visit was Savoie—if he was even there, at all. The fair Doyle would have to crash the plan, and save Callie from herself.

She paused, much struck, because this was exactly what she always did for Acton—crash his plan, so as to save him from himself. Mayhap it ran in the family.

When they arrived at their destination, Doyle suggested, "Why don't you come up, Adrian?" This, because Acton would be just as unhappy with his wife, if she wandered anywhere without an escort, and it wouldn't surprise her if her husband was already taking a long look at her GPS, and wondering why she'd gone over to Mary's, so unexpectedly.

"Yes, ma'am," Adrian agreed, and then said little else, as they began to walk toward the building's main door.

Callie's going to know that he grassed her out, Doyle realized. Poor Adrian; but he did the right thing, in telling me —best to err on the side of caution.

Doyle's phone pinged, and she saw that it was Reynolds. Here's another one, she thought, who's wondering why Callie broke security protocols to come over with Edward; the poor lass is not going to redeem herself, anytime soon, in the butler's eyes.

"Ho, Reynolds," she said in a cheerful tone. "Adrian and I were just comin' up—we're on the pavement below."

"Oh—oh, madam; such a relief. Is Edward with you?"

For a moment, Doyle's heart stilled. "Isn't he there with you?"

"No, madam; Mr. Savoie rang me up, just now, and said he thought he saw Miss Callie with Master Edward, walking on the pavement below. I phoned Mr. Trenton, but I couldn't raise him."

Tamping down her concern, Doyle's gaze swept the shops along the street. Callie wouldn't be doing anything to harm Edward—she knew it down to the soles of her shoes. The trusty ice cream shop was a block away—mayhap they'd stopped to get a treat, before going up to Mary's. "I'll look for them, Reynolds; keep trying to raise Trenton."

There was a small pause. "I feel I should call Lord Acton, madam."

Doyle closed her eyes, briefly. "Aye. But make sure to tell him I'm here, and that I'm not over-worried."

Doyle rang off, and then said to Adrian, "They're likely at the ice-cream shop; we'll start there."

"Yes, ma'am."

They began to walk in that direction, Doyle doing her best to hurry. There's a perfectly innocent explanation, she told herself stubbornly, but faith, am I going to give that girl a righteous bear-garden jawing, about not haring-off and doing whatever she feels, just because she's that annoyed with all of us.

They came to the ice cream shop, and Doyle stayed Adrian with a hand, as she reconnoitered through the window—it was always best to do a survey, first.

"There they are," Adrian declared in a relieved tone, as he pointed. "Toward the back, see?"

"Holy *Mother*," Doyle breathed. They were there, indeed, but they were not alone. Seated at one of the little round tables that were scattered in the back of the shop was Doyle's false Aunty, a squirming Edward on her lap, since the woman was holding him a little too tightly.

With acute dismay, Doyle assessed the tableau before her, noting that Callie hovered beside the woman, clearly uneasy.

She's realized this is not good, thought Doyle, but she's not sure how alarmed she should be, and what she should do. Fortunately, the calvary's about to crash-in to the rescue.

She said to Adrian in a low voice, "I know that woman, and she may be dangerous. Have you a gun?"

This was an educated guess, being as Acton-of-the illegal-stockpile would presumably arm anyone who was regularly tasked with escorting the fair Doyle.

Nonplussed, her companion didn't respond immediately, and Doyle said, with a touch of impatience, "Hand it over, please; I don't have mine."

"I don't know as I should, ma'am," he admitted.

Rather than remind him that she was a police officer—albeit a grossly pregnant one—she recalibrated her plan. "All right, then—I don't know as I'm in any shape to take her down, anyways. Instead, I'll go in all friendly-like, and as soon as I am close to them, you'll create a distraction in the doorway. I'll grab Edward, and you'll come-in to take her down. Don't be kind; get her to the ground as quickly as you can, and cover her, if you have to—she may be armed."

"Yes, ma'am," he said, ably hiding his alarm.

Taking a breath, Doyle pinned on a smile, and came through the doors, waving at the huddled group as she approached then with an easy pace. "There you are! I thought as much."

Callie jumped guiltily, as well she should, but Doyle just chuckled, as she casually made her way closer. "I was wondering why you'd come over here—Edward has a GPS device, sewn into his clothes." This was made-up, but Doyle knew it was easily believable, for anyone with a passing knowledge of Acton.

"Mum!" said Edward with much relief, being as he didn't much like being constrained on this stranger's lap.

But Wickham only emanated acute dismay, as she rose to

her feet, hoisting the child up on a hip, and backing away. "Oh
—" she said; "Oh, Kathleen; I didn't expect you."

Nervously, she glanced toward the door, and Doyle
immediately stepped to block her line of vision.

"I'll have an ice cream, too," Doyle declared brightly, and
held out a hand. "Come, Edward; let's go choose—we'll get
one for everyone."

But with an abrupt movement, the woman twisted Edward
away from Doyle's reaching hands. "No—no, not yet; let me
hold him a bit longer—"

"Nobody moves!" Adrian shouted at the door, as he walked
in, with his gun drawn menacingly. "This is a robbery—
everyone down on the floor."

CHAPTER 37

The assorted customers exclaimed in dismay, and Doyle shouted in her best police-officer voice, "Quickly; we should do what he says."

"Who is *he*?" Wickham said in confusion, still clutching Edward in an iron grip. "He's not supposed—"

"Mr. Adrian!" Edward exclaimed, in astonished delight.

Adrian ignored the little boy, and instead barked, "Nobody moves! Show me your hands, and get down!"

"Quickly," urged Callie, who was well-aware that Adrian wouldn't be acting the brigand, without good reason. Gently, she tugged at Edward. "Let me take him; we don't want him to get hurt."

But the woman was reluctant to loosen her hold on Edward, and instead stepped back, clearly confused—which was just as well, since Doyle was not at all sure she could manage to get herself down on the floor, without tipping over. With her own hands up, she warned Wickham, "It's best not to resist—just do what he asks. Put your hands up."

Enjoying himself immensely, Edward promptly raised his hands to the ceiling, but unfortunately, his captor did not follow suit.

But Doyle had been doing a covert assessment, and had decided that the woman was not armed. If push comes to shove, she decided, I'll knock her down; I just need to get close enough to put a leg behind hers—I outweigh her, after all.

"Just take everything," said the cashier, who'd opened the cash drawer, and stepped back, with his hands up. "Don't scare everyone—no call for that, mate."

"Bang!" shouted Edward, obviously hoping for gunplay.

But then things took an unexpected turn, as Savoie strode into the shop, and then was brought up short on the threshold, as he observed Adrian, holding everyone at gunpoint.

Nonplussed, Adrian managed to say in a menacing tone, "You! Stay where you are; show me your hands."

"Best do as he says," Doyle called out, so that the Frenchman would know she was there.

"Mr. Sad-wa!" Edward shouted in excitement, "Mr. Adrian is going to shoot us!"

Savoie turned to Adrian, and held out his hand, palm up. "Give it to me," he said.

Doyle could hear the other customers gasp at this supposed show of courage, but she was more worried about the fact that Adrian was unlikely to surrender his weapon, and so—to ward off a tussle—she called out to Adrian, "Yes; shame on you, for frightenin' everyone—there are children present."

Hearing her, Savoie jerked his head toward the door. "Go."

"Aye; begone," Doyle called out.

But yet again, circumstances took an unexpected turn, as Acton himself stepped through the door behind Savoie, his own weapon aimed at Adrian. "Police," he announced. "No one moves."

"It's that famous detective," a woman to Doyle's right whispered, in an excited tone.

"That's my da," Edward explained proudly.

With an air of defeat, Wickham allowed the little boy to slide to the floor.

CHAPTER 38

*A*drian had been duly cuffed, and seated in the corner of the shop, and then Acton released the witnesses, explaining to the cashier that he wouldn't be needed to give a statement, since police personnel had witnessed the crime.

"That's a right shame," said the cashier, who nodded in admiration toward Savoie. "Make sure to say this chap was brilliant; I think he surprised him—shook him up."

"I do the shooking," Savoie agreed, accepting this accolade with a modest bow of his head. "Many times."

"I will be in touch," said Acton to the Frenchman, in a dismissive tone.

Why, Acton's that angry at Savoie, Doyle realized, as the other man took his leave. But he shouldn't be; Savoie did indeed save the day—Savoie and Adrian, between them. Acton's probably annoyed that they allowed a live weapon in the same room as his wife and son. That, or he's annoyed that it wasn't him, saving the day—and heaven save us, from alpha-males.

Her scalp prickled, but before she would contemplate why it would, Acton suggested that she and Edward be seated with Adrian, whilst he went to speak with Callie and Aunty Wickham.

"Should I take off your cuffs?" Doyle asked Adrian, as she settled-in beside him. "Oh, never mind—I haven't my kit; we'll have to wait for Acton."

The young man shrugged. "That's all right, ma'am—although I will say it feels a bit creepy."

"A reminder to commit no major crimes," she advised.

"Right, ma'am. Am I going to the police station?"

"No. And good work, you—very resourceful." Doyle wasn't sure it had been the best idea to wave a weapon around in a public place—since you never knew how people might react—but it had all ended without bloodshed—thank God fastin'—and so there was little point in second-guessing.

"You're a robber," Edward observed with wonder, mixed with a tinge of admiration.

Adrian grinned. "Not really, Edward; I was just pretending."

"Can I feel your hair?"

Doyle and Adrian both chuckled, because the young man had removed his driver's hat to play his part, and now his dreadlocks were on full display.

Firmly, Doyle pulled the little boy's hand down. "No Edward, you may not. Mind yourself, please."

"May I have an ice cream?" the little boy asked next, with a wistful glance at the flavors that were on display, behind the glass case.

Doyle blew out a breath. "We all deserve a massive ice cream, but let's wait—we can't be havin' ice cream, whilst poor Mr. Adrian sits here in cuffs. You may go over to look in the case, though, and think about which flavor you'll have."

Adrian watched Acton, as he spoke to the others, and asked quietly, "Is he going to arrest her?"

"No," Doyle replied.

"Because of Callie."

"Because of Callie," she agreed.

He turned to Doyle, and ventured, "Is that woman not right in the head, or something?"

"I'm not sure," Doyle said honestly, and then added, "but we know that she's a con-artist."

He made a soft, whistling sound. "Poor Callie—this has got to sting. I'm surprised Lord Acton is so calm."

Calm, like a volcano, Doyle thought, as she watched her husband speaking quietly to the two women.

Acton rose, and approached Adrian, to release his cuffs. "If you will drive Miss Callie home, please. I will take Lady Acton and Edward home."

"Yes, sir."

Not a bad move, thought Doyle, as the pale-lipped girl silently passed before them, and accompanied the young man out the door. Adrian will be sympathetic, even as he scolds her. They go back a long ways, after all.

"Wait—mum said we can have ice cream," Edward said in all anxiety, as his father took his hand, and turned to leave.

"On the house," the cashier announced, and so they paused to order their treats—even Acton, which did not in any way fool his wife, as to the state of her husband's frame-of-mind.

To walk him back from the ledge, Doyle offered, "I think my

wretched Aunty was waitin' for Charbonneau—she kept lookin' at the door, as though she was expectin' someone to come in."

"Perhaps," he replied, as he thanked the cashier, and they headed out the door.

In a practical manner, she added, "It didn't seem like an abduction, Michael—else she wouldn't have met Callie in such a public place. More likely Edward was just the excuse, so that Charbonneau could come on-site, and use the opportunity to threaten Callie, or mayhap enlist her, in some scheme."

"You may be right," he agreed.

Faith, he's simmering, and nearly a'boil, Doyle thought, as she continued, "And now we see the reason my false Aunty was sent-in, on this ridiculous charade. We thought she was trying to winkle me, but the whole time she was winklin' Callie, who was ripe for it, and already feelin' that the world was a very unjust place."

"I would not disagree," he said, and took another bite of his ice cream.

Now, that's interesting, thought Doyle, as she took her own bite. He's resorted to backwards-speak, because I think he knows something—or at least, he suspects something that he's not telling me. Mayhap he's covering for Callie, and doesn't want me to know what was actually planned—which is a bit ominous. I don't like to think what could have gone wrong— we were lucky, that Savoie gave Reynolds the head's up, and then came along, when he did.

Her scalp prickled, and she paused. This did seem a bit too convenient—that Savoie happened to spot the two, when they were on the loose. More likely that the Frenchman had become aware of Charbonneau's plan, somehow, and was planning on confronting the wretched woman at the ice-cream shop. It would also explain why Acton was that angry; he suspected that Savoie knew what was planned, and was going to handle Charbonneau himself, without telling him. After all, Savoie was affiliated with Charbonneau, in some way—she'd never discovered exactly how.

Doyle took another bite of her ice cream, and decided this seemed the most likely explanation for her husband's epic bad mood; Savoie was going to sweep this little episode under the rug, with Acton none the wiser, and such a plan would not sit well with her husband—not with his wife and child at risk. So; it looked like the Frenchman was slated to hear a righteous bear-garden jawing, himself.

They came to the car, and then paused so as to allow Edward to make a bit more progress on his treat before strapping him in the Range Rover—a lesson learned, the hard way.

Doyle bent to clean-up Edward's cone, licking the sides, before handing it back to him. "Where's our Trenton? No one could raise him."

"Trenton is conducting a sting operation, and so he is not answering calls."

She glanced up in surprise. "What sort of sting?"

Her husband explained, "He is posing as a middleman from Bristol, who'd been shorted on an illegal transaction. It is an attempt to lure Charbonneau's allies into making damaging statements."

Doyle nodded, and immediately drew her own conclusions. If Trenton was the lure, it seemed obvious that this was not a CID-sanctioned exercise, which only made sense, after all. Acton's plan to use Rosanna had failed, and so now he'd come up with another plan, so as to obtain leverage over the blacklegs. Above all, he wanted to force them to step down without having anyone delve too deeply into the details of the skimming rig—being as those details might implicate a certain Chief Inspector.

Following this line of thought, Doyle observed with some alarm, "Faith, Michael—it can't be a coincidence, that Aunty Wickham talked Callie into bringing Edward over, just as Trenton would be unavailable. It looks as though Charbonneau knew what you were about, with Trenton's sting operation."

"I cannot disagree," he replied.

More backwards-speak, she noted, as she bent to wipe Edward's sticky hands; it looks as though my husband was outfoxed, in this instance, and small wonder, that he's furious —such a thing doesn't happen very often.

She straightened up, and laid a calming hand on his arm. "You'll come about, my friend; these paltry bureaucrats have no idea what they're up against. But please be careful, Michael; I know you think you can out-dance the devil himself, but don't forget to count the cost."

"I won't," he replied, as he lifted Edward into the car. "Believe me."

CHAPTER 39

essage received, he thought a bit grimly, and arranged for a cease-fire.

The following afternoon, Doyle went for the usual playground-visit with Edward, and was delighted to see that this time, Mary had accompanied Savoie and the children; pushing a pram, with baby Hannah carefully tucked within.

A breakthrough, thought Doyle, who greeted the other young woman warmly. "Such a fine day, Mary; it's good to see you out."

"Do you see my sister, Lady Acton?" Gemma interrupted excitedly, her hand on the pram. "She's sleeping, now, but she should wake, soon."

"She's lovely, Gemma; truly."

"She can't smile yet, but mum says she smiles at me with

her eyes." Reaching in, she gently patted the sleeping baby. "Mr. Savoie calls her *"chou-chou."*

"That's French, I would guess," said Doyle.

Gemma nodded. "Emile knows more French than I do. I'm going to catch up, and then we will both know Russian and French."

"My hat's off to you," Doyle replied; "I barely know English."

"Come on, Gemma—hurry up," Emile called out, from the ladder.

"Emile," warned Savoie, who then assumed his usual post, at the playground's edge.

Mary smiled. "Go ahead, Gemma—I'll have a chat with Lady Acton."

With a final, beaming glance at the baby, the little girl whirled around, and ran off.

Once she was out of earshot, Mary turned to Doyle with a warm smile. "I have wonderful news—I've just heard that Gemma's adoption has gone through."

"Oh—oh, *finally*. I'm that happy for you, Mary."

"Philippe thinks that we should hold a party for her, but I'm not sure whether I want to; Gemma's not really aware that it was even a concern."

"I can see that," Doyle agreed. "No need to rake up any confusion, or remind her that Hannah's not truly her sister."

Mary nodded, as they watched Gemma follow Emile, across the bridgeway to the slide. "It's such a blessing," she said softly. "Such good news; I'd forgot what it was like—to be happy."

She blinked away tears, and Doyle put a fond arm around

her, and squeezed. "In all things, give thanks—at least that's what the Apostle said. It's not always easy, though, is it?"

"No," Mary agreed, and took a steadying breath. "We can only have faith that everything is meant for a purpose."

"Again, not always easy," Doyle admitted. "I suppose it's just as well that I'm not the one in charge."

They watched Savoie approach, to see if he'd left his sunglasses on the bench, but they weren't there.

"You should put them on a string 'round your neck, like Gemma's mittens," Mary teased. "You're always losing them, Philippe."

Remembering what Father John had said, Doyle covertly watched Savoie interact with Mary, but she couldn't catch any leap of emotion, on the Frenchman's part. Instead, they seemed merely good friends, who were comfortable with each other— although that was extraordinary enough, that sweet Mary would be so comfortable, with a man like Savoie.

I'll believe it when I see it, Doyle decided, as she watched him walk back to his post, shielding his eyes from the afternoon sun. I may not know Savoie as well as I know Acton, but I know him fairly well, and it beggars belief, that he'd take a submissive role in a courtship, waiting patiently in the background. That's not his style, at all—he's as much a take-no-prisoners sort of person as Acton is. And—to be fair—it's very hard for the female heart to resist a take-no-prisoners sort of person.

Suddenly struck, she realized that there was another reason she found this supposed romance so hard to believe; he'd a full measure of undeniable sex-appeal, had Philippe Savoie, but he was not playing that card with Mary—not even a hint of it. So; mayhap Father John was wrong, and Savoie's only motivation, in helping-out the widow, was to keep Emile's found-family from moving away. That would be miles more in keeping, since the man's son meant everything to him.

And, thought Doyle; speaking of sons that mean everything, I should thank Savoie for his actions, yesterday. He may be many things, but at least he is willing to come to the rescue, and then be discreet about it—a lesson I learned, literally, the first time I met him.

Doyle rose to her feet, and wandered over to chat with Reynolds for a moment, as he and Edward made a fortress in the sand, and then she casually walked over to stand beside Savoie.

"I wanted to thank you, Philippe," she offered. "I don't know what Callie was thinkin', to kick over the traces like that. Hopefully, it was a hard lesson learned."

Carelessly, he replied, "*De rien,*" and seemed disinclined to discuss it.

With a mental sigh, Doyle decided she shouldn't let him "discreet" it away, and so she persisted, "I hope she hasn't been makin' a pest of herself, Philippe. She's young, and a bit silly, sometimes."

"*Non-non,*" he assured her, with a thoroughly Gallic shrug, but this was not exactly true.

Oh-oh, Doyle thought; he's too much of a gentleman to say that Callie's been pestering him. Or, mayhap, it's not necessarily that he's a gentleman, but he can't very well muddy the Acton-waters by snubbing the man's love-lorn sister. I should have been paying more attention to all of this, but in my defense, I've been ministering to poor Mary, and I haven't had time to deal with anyone else's troubles—hers took priority.

And then—as though on cue—Doyle spotted Callie

approaching, her hands in her pockets and her cheeks a bit pale.

Diplomatically, Doyle moved away from Savoie, and walked over to greet the girl. "Callie; have you recovered from your scoldin?"

The young woman took a resolute breath. "I've come to apologize to you, Lady Acton. Dr. Tim came to visit, and told me it was important that I make amends—he said he has to apologize to you, too."

But Doyle only made a face. "Fah, Callie; the woman was a hardened con-artist, and neither one of you has a single thing to be ashamed of. A good con-artist can pick your pocket whilst singin' the *Ave Maria*."

Callie admitted, "It was the accent, I think—it was so like yours. Your accent sounds—I don't know; it automatically sounds so *honest*, I suppose."

"Does it? Well, fancy that." Diplomatically, Doyle didn't volunteer to tell the girl how an English accent sounded, to Irish ears. "Come on; let's sit down together."

They were seated on the next bench from Mary's, and Callie glanced over, asking in an anxious tone, "Does Miss Mary know what happened?"

"She does not," Doyle said. "The only people who know are Savoie and Adrian, and neither one of them is the sort to bring down disgrace upon your head." She paused. "You're lucky, in your friends."

Callie nodded, her gaze falling to her hands, resting in her lap. "I know. Adrian scolded me—told me I was stupid, to let it get that far."

Philosophically, Doyle nodded. "A lot of people we see, in our business, get into trouble because they're too embarrassed to make a scene. Next time, knock the table over, and shout for help; the more eyes that are on you, the better."

The girl nodded, and lifted her head to meet Doyle's gaze. "I am so sorry, Lady Acton. You know I would never harm Edward."

Doyle said only, "I will say that when Acton warns you away from somethin', know that he means it. He's very good, at what he does."

"I suppose I didn't like that he was telling me what to do," she admitted in a subdued tone, and her eyes rested on Savoie, for a moment.

"Well, Acton's a bossy thing, but he's usually right," Doyle observed. "I've learned that lesson myself, many a time."

The girl lowered her gaze, and then said, with a burst of emotion, "I'm so ashamed—everything's gone wrong."

But Doyle wasn't having it, since on the next bench over sat a young woman who had a far better claim, to that particular lament. "No, Callie; that's where you're wrong—everything's happenin' exactly as it's supposed to. You're havin' your day of adversity, just like the Psalmist says, but you can't truly expect to walk through life without sustaining a few hard knocks— that's not the way it works. Instead, it's how you react to those knocks, that's what's important. So what, if you were a gooseberry-baby? Faith, so was I. You can't live a life of resentment, over something you'd no control over. Instead, thank God fastin' that you're alive and well, and that you'd good people, to see you to adulthood."

Callie nodded, as she bowed her head to surreptitiously wipe away tears with her fingertips.

Doyle laid a hand on her arm, and squeezed in sympathy as they sat together in silence, for a few minutes. I don't know what I was so worried about, she thought; there's nothin' to this "sistering" business, after all.

Gently teasing, Doyle asked, "So; I'm slated to hear an apology from Tim McGonigal, too? This may take all afternoon."

"Yes—he feels dreadful about it."

Doyle made a sound of impatience. "He oughtn't—he's the perfect mark, since he's too kind to recognize a conniver, when he sees one."

Her companion mustered up a smile. "I suppose that's true."

"No harm done, and we should all move on, rather than dwell on past mistakes."

"Thank you, Lady Acton."

"Kathleen," Doyle reminded her.

"Kathleen," Callie dutifully offered.

Savoie came over, to take his leave. "I go," he announced, and checked the time. "I have the meeting."

"I will transport Master Emile over to Miss Mary's, for his homework," Reynolds assured him.

"Emile," Savoie called out. "You must mind Monsieur Reynolds."

"Right, Papa," the boy called back.

Doyle watched Savoie walk away, his hands thrust into his pockets, and thought, he seems happy—his mood is much lighter, than it has been. This business with Gemma must have been weighing on him, too.

CHAPTER 40

$\mathcal{I}$n a conciliatory gesture, he'd offered to go over to the Frenchman's flat, and then, once they were seated, he spoke in French, which was another conciliatory gesture. "I have been maladroit, and I must apologize."

"De rien," Savoie replied in his negligent manner, his expression impassive.

"Believe me, when I say that I did not mean to offend."

"This is no offense—it is forgotten," Savoie assured him.

"I feel I have little choice, but to proceed with the case against the Public Accounts Commission. Fortunately, most do not know of our involvement."

"Oui," his companion agreed.

"Two are aware, however. The Committee Chair, and Ms. Charbonneau."

Savoie nodded. "You take one, I will take the other."

"Merci," he said politely. And now, do we disengage our business pursuits?"

"Non," said Savoie, showing a hint of surprise that such a thing would be suggested. "We are men; we do not nurse our resentments, like women."

"Bien," Acton agreed, as he offered his hand, and was glad his wife wasn't present, to hear this particular lie.

CHAPTER 41

*D*oyle was having another lie-down, being as she had to pace herself more and more, lately—the spirit was willing, but the flesh felt like it was dragging around a sack of wet cement.

She hadn't realized that she'd fallen asleep, until she was facing Bill Blakney again—the ghost having a chuckle, at her expense. "Look at you."

"Don't remind me—at least it will be over, soon."

"Back to how it should be," he agreed, and seemed very pleased.

Fairly, she noted, "Life's a bit different, nowadays. It's a strange thing, to always be goin' from a playground, to a crime scene, and then back again. It's as though I have a foot in in two completely different worlds."

"Not so different," said the ghost, and cocked a brow at her.

She thought this over. "I suppose you can see the same interactions in both—the same roles being played, and the same squabbles. We can hear the echoes from the playground loud and clear, throughout the rest of our lives—I'll give you that."

He nodded. "All's well that ends well."

She smiled. "Aye—for both of us. Acton's not goin' to prison—not that I ever doubted the man, of course. And Gemma's not goin' back to Russia; it looks like the both of us were frettin' about nothin'."

He seemed amused, but only said, "Good luck, to you."

"Don't be a stranger," she replied. "Who's goin' to tell me to mind my own business? Acton would rather fall on a sword—even though I know he wishes I would, sometimes."

"Ha—you never listen to me, why should you listen to him?"

She smiled. "That's a good point. I guess I'm yet another one, who'd rather take my own advice."

"Speaking of advice, try to keep Edward away from a girl named Gina, at university," the ghost warned.

Doyle blinked. "Right. I hope I remember."

Thinking on this, the ghost made a thoroughly masculine sound of appreciation. "Although there's another one, I wouldn't turn down."

"You're dead," Doyle reminded him with a smile. "Off you go."

She opened her eyes, and rolled over to check the time—dinner, soon; she could smell something cooking. The nursery monitor was on, and faintly, she could hear Callie reading to Edward—*The Gingerbread Man*, of course; poor Peter Rabbit had been given short shrift.

Sliding out of bed, she walked down the hall to her husband's office; he'd been called-out to a homicide scene, earlier—another high-level case—and she wanted to hear if there were any updates.

Just as she approached his office door, he came out, and saw her approaching. "I was coming to check on you," he said, and drew her into an embrace. "How are you feeling?"

"Miserable," she replied, and rested her cheek against his chest. "But I'm agog to hear the latest report."

This, because the Chair of the Public Accounts Commission had committed suicide—which was not much of a surprise, all in all; the CID had started arresting some of the lower-level suspects, and it was only a matter of time before the Chair's own role in the scandal became clear.

Still, the CID had to make sure his cohorts hadn't decided to silence him, and so Acton had been called-in to process the scene. It seemed cut-and-dried, though; a classic locked-door case, where the man had hung himself from a light fixture, alone in his posh home.

"I am just finishing my report," he advised. "We'll wait for a tox-screen, but it certainly appears to be suicide-by-hanging."

She let out a breath. "Well, suicide's a sin, but you almost can't blame him. The walls were closin' in, and he was facin' a tidal wave of disgrace—not to mention it won't be very hard to connect the dots to the tainted-medication case, and poor Nigel Howard's death."

"So, it would seem," Acton agreed.

She tilted her head back to look up at him. "Has anyone fingered Charbonneau, yet?"

"There is very little implicating evidence, with regard to Charbonneau."

She lowered her head to his chest, again. "Aye, she's a

slippery one. And—speakin' of slippery ones—I will say that I'm that relieved no one has hauled you away in cuffs."

"Yet," he teased.

"Yet. I haven't the energy to deliver a lecture, just now, so you can think about what I would blister you about, and we can just skip that part."

"This is an unexpected boon," he said, and kissed the top of her head. "Many thanks."

She chuckled, and he chuckled, and she thought—I'm massive, 'round the middle, and he's so much taller, but somehow, we always fit together perfectly. Just like that ying-and-yams thing.

Into the contented silence, she offered, "I've finally realized, husband, that you always stay one step ahead of the headsman because that's how you like it—it's bred into your very bones. I may be a bit dim, but at least I've figured that out—Edward didn't get his buccaneerin' ways from nowhere."

But, as usual, he gave one of his patented non-answers, as his hands moved gently on her back. "I do regret causing you distress. On my honor, Kathleen."

"Well, I think you did a fair bit of distressin' yourself, for this one—it was a close-run thing. I realize that you can't be happy unless you're plottin' to send out a raidin' party—just like your wretched ancestors—but recall that things didn't always go so well for them, either. It's that Greek-pride thing—what's the word?"

"Hubris?"

"Aye, that's it. Faith, those wretched Greek play-writers would have a field day, if they tried to write down your life, in three parts."

"This part is—by far—the best part."

She reached to kiss his throat, in appreciation. "Never had a nicer time, I assure you."

They were both disinclined to move, and so continued to stand in a fond embrace, as Reynolds came down the steps to announce dinner, saw them, and then did an abrupt about-face, back up the stairs.

"Who's gettin' arrested next?" she asked.

"Everyone who deserves it," he replied. "And then, I imagine reforms will be suggested, so that such a thing never happens again."

But she only made a skeptical sound, into his shirtfront. "It's always the same old song, Michael; unless you can recruit a commission of saints, there's always going to be a weak reed, or two. The problem with temptation is that it is so very, very tempting—although I suppose I'm preachin' to the choir, to mention such a thing."

"Believe me, when I say that I do not take what has happened here lightly."

There was a grim determination, 'neath his words, and reminded, she asked, "Would you mind dispatchin' Munoz, to go and tell Yessenia's mum, once everyone's been rolled-up? She can see what her daughter set in motion, and be proud of her. She'd rather have her daughter back, of course, but at least, its somethin'."

"You don't wish to tell her yourself?"

"No; Munoz should handle it—I think it will help her mind, a bit. She's carryin' around a bucketful of guilt."

"And speaking of guilt, McGonigal phoned, and was wondering if we would come over for dinner, tomorrow. Shall I put him off?"

She made a sound of impatience. "Faith, yes—he just wants

249

to apologize, and I'm pig-sick of everyone apologizin' to me. Although you can ask him if he remembers how to deliver babies—I imagine they taught him, back in medical school."

Slowly, Acton lifted his head. "You don't want Dr. Easton to attend Tommy's birth?"

"Dr. Easton is not my doctor, Michael; Dr. Easton is your doctor."

With his hands on her arms, he stepped away, so that he could look into her face, his expression one of concern. "He is very well-regarded, Kathleen."

She lifted her chin. "Not by me."

Nonplussed, her husband ventured, "I am not certain the hospital will allow McGonigal privileges, so as to attend a childbirth."

"Fine," she declared. "I'll have him 'attend a childbirth' here. Hospitals give me the willies, anyways."

There was a small silence, whilst his thumbs brushed her arms. "What if there is an emergency?"

With all confidence, she replied, "There won't be—this is Tommy, we're talkin' about; he's no trouble a'tall."

Her husband bowed his head in concession. "If you insist, then. I will raise the subject, when I give McGonigal our regrets."

"Good," she said, and then braced her hands against her back. "Best do it within the next hour, or so."

EPILOGUE

"*S*uch a shame," said Charbonneau, as she lay in the
tousled sheets, close against him. They were taking a
breather, before gearing up for another round of sex; smoking
cigarettes, as they watched the rain patter against the window.

"*Oui*," he agreed.

She smiled to herself, as she drew on the cigarette. He was never
one to talk, much. She'd been a bit worried that he was no longer
interested—she hadn't heard from him, lately—but today he'd come
'round to see her, unannounced. It was rather sweet, really; he must
have known that she was a bit spooked, with everything that was
going on. And it was reassuring, too—she'd been worried that she
could no longer count on his protection. She'd been seriously thinking
about going somewhere to lie low, and then—such a relief—he'd
shown up, at her door.

She blew out a stream of smoke. "I should have known that she
was too jumpy, to pull it off, but we needed someone Irish." She
sighed. "I should have trusted my instincts."

She moved her head, to glance up at him. "Are you worried about her?"

"Non," he said, and drew on his cigarette. "You must not worry, chérie."

She ventured, "Well, you keep telling me that he's not going to go after me, but I'm not so sure. He's got a lot of influence."

Tilting his head in acknowledgement, he admitted, "Oui."

This was a bit concerning, and so she frowned slightly. "Maybe I should leave town for a while—just to be cautious."

He thought this over, as he exhaled, and watched the rain for a few seconds. "We can go to la belle France, peut-être."

She propped herself on an elbow, to look upon him in surprise. "You'd go, too?"

He smiled at her reaction. "Oui; I have not been home, in some time."

Unable to suppress a smile, she said, "That sounds wonderful— I'd love to see your home-town."

He explained, "I cannot go, so much, because I am on the lists, for the police. But if we sail there, I avoid the lists. I know men in Bristol, who have the sailboats."

"Smugglers?" she teased, still pleased beyond measure that he would want to take a trip with her. "I'm not surprised."

He raised his brows. "I do not ask them what they do, and they do not ask me what I do."

She laughed aloud. "That sounds lovely—so romantic. We won't take that little boy of yours, will we? There's not a lot of privacy, when he's around."

"Non-non," he assured her, and reached to stroke her hair. "Me and you, seulement."

She leaned to kiss his ear, lingeringly. "Sounds like heaven," she murmured. May as well make it clear that he'd be rewarded for this invitation, and many times over. It was rather thrilling, really—he must like her more than he let on.

"D'accord—I will arrange for it." With a smile, he tapped his cigarette ash into the ashtray.